Email 英語
會話與寫作技巧
How to Write Email in English

David Shih ／著

哈福

史上最佳英文E-mail寫作指南

　　國際村時代來臨，能用流暢英語寫好email已成為職場致勝關鍵、交友的必備秘密武器。

　　在網路資訊豐富的年代裡，人們已經以email取代了郵件、電報、傳真、電話等傳統通訊方式，其低廉的成本及高效率的通訊，已成為日常生活中不可或 的一部份。因此，確實掌握英語email，已經成為現代人的必要課題。

　　也許你認為email只是寫出一封信而已，但不同於傳統書信的寫法，email重視的是速度與效率；因此，與一般的英文寫作不同的是：一封好的email應該行文簡潔，以簡短有力的文字表達出最精準確實的訊息，並在往返的信件中，取得彼此之間的共識與溝通。

　　這本《**Email英語會話與寫作技巧**》，為讀者整理出所有email操作上的必備詞彙與用語，你雖然可能常在使用email，但是你知道主機、游標、附加檔案、收件匣、寄件匣的英文怎麼說嗎？透過文中輕鬆的生活會話，期望提供讀者一個更了解email機會，同時幫助你在生活、課業與工作上靈活運用。

本書三大特色

1. 豐富內容・精采實用

　　本書分十章共三十單元，從最基本的電腦開機，到了解

2

電腦的操作，各項的功能介紹應有盡有，一步步讓你了解收發email的基本技巧。各單元完全針對電腦生手的需要編寫，以最生動有趣的方式來呈現主題，讓您在最輕鬆愉快的氣氛下，達到事半功倍的學習效果。

2. 精選單字‧課後練習

本書整理出收發email時的相關實用字彙，配合對話的內容，使您在充實英文字彙的同時，也能有效靈活運用在日常會話之中。另外，每篇文章之後皆附完整課後練習題，幫助個人檢視學習效果。

3. 專業錄音‧輕鬆學習

針對全書內容，特聘專業美籍錄音師錄製朗讀MP3，發音標準、音質純正，與本書搭配學習，使您在學會email技巧的同時，也能學習到純正道地的英語發音，英語會話能力迅速提升！

無論你平常較少接觸電腦，或者已具備電腦基礎，相信透過本書step by step的教學內容，都能夠滿足你對email英文知識的好奇，並且在生活中靈活運用，本書希望能夠幫助每位朋友在課業、職場或人際溝通方面能更上一層樓！相信此刻的你，一定迫不及待想了解這本書，趕快跟隨書中內容一同輕鬆學習，相信很快的，你也可以成為一位email高手喔！

編者 謹識

Chapter
1
Chapter
2
Chapter
3
Chapter
4
Chapter
5
Chapter
6
Chapter
7
Chapter
8
Chapter
9
Chapter
10

目錄

Chapter 1
Chapter 2
Chapter 3
Chapter 4
Chapter 5
Chapter 6
Chapter 7
Chapter 8
Chapter 9
Chapter 10

Chapter 1
Chapter 2
Chapter 3
Chapter 4
Chapter 5
Chapter 6
Chapter 7
Chapter 8
Chapter 9
Chapter 10

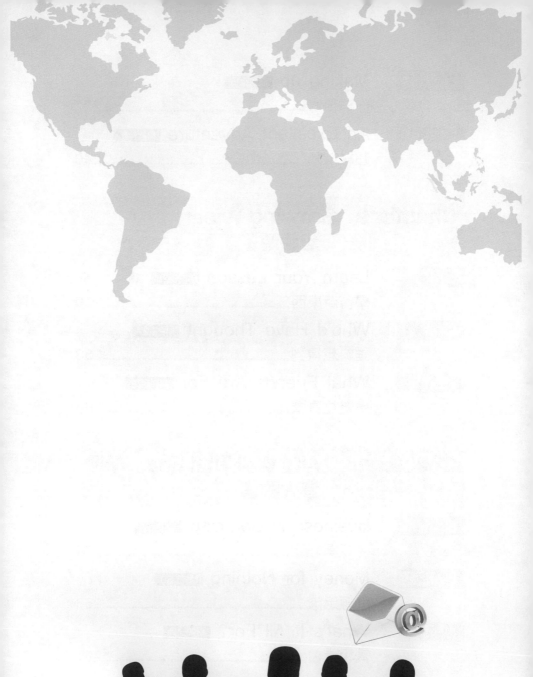

Chapter

1

Ready to Begin

開麥拉

Unit 1　Help
小幫手

Ted is sitting in front of a computer in Kara's house.
泰德坐在卡拉屋裡的電腦前。

👤 Ted泰德　　👤 Kara卡拉

Ted: Kara,will you come in here, please?
卡拉，妳進來一下好嗎？

Kara: Where are you, Ted?
你在哪裡呀，泰德？

Ted: I'm in the office, sitting at the computer.
我在辦公室的電腦這裡。

Kara: You never use the computer. What are you doing?
你從來不用電腦的，你在那邊幹嘛？

Ted: I want to send an email. I need you to help me.
我想發一封電子郵件，需要你幫我。

Chapter
1

Chapter
2

Chapter
3

Chapter
4

Chapter
5

Chapter
6

Chapter
7

Chapter
8

Chapter
9

Chapter
10

> Kara comes in.
> 卡拉走了進來。

Kara: Ted, you haven't turned the computer on.
泰德,你連電腦都還沒開機呢。

Ted: Oh.
哦。

Kara: Well, it would help if you turned it on. You know how to turn it on, don't you?
如果電腦是開的,就沒問題了,你會開機吧?

Ted: Well, I don't use a computer at work.
呃,我上班時不用電腦。

Kara: That's right. You are a tree planter.
沒錯,你是種樹的。

Ted: Right. There are no computers in the forest.
是啊,森林裡沒有電腦。

Kara: Okay. Press this button on the computer tower.
好,按一下電腦直立主機上的這個按鈕。

Ted: Why do you call it a "tower"? It's more

like a box.

妳為什麼叫它「直立主機」？它比較像是個盒子。

Kara: I don't know why it is called a tower. It just is.

我也不知道為什麼叫直立主機，反正就是這樣叫。

Ted: Okay. What else?

好吧，然後呢？

Kara: Press this button on the monitor.

按一下顯示器上的這個按鈕。

Ted: Why is it called a monitor? It doesn't monitor anything.

為什麼它叫顯示器？它又沒有顯示誰。

Kara: Ted, do you want my help or not?

泰德，你到底要不要我幫忙？

Ted: Yes, I want you to help me.

要啦，我需要妳的幫忙。

Kara: Okay, then. This is called a computer tower and you press this button to turn it on.

來，這是電腦直立主機，你按下這個按鈕就可以開機。

Ted: Okay.
好的。

Kara: And this is called a monitor and you press this button to turn it on.
這是顯示器，你按一下這個鈕就可以打開顯示器。

Ted: Now what do we do?
然後要做什麼呢？

Kara: Now the computer is ready to go.
現在你就可以開始用電腦了。

Ted: So now what do we do?
再來要做什麼呢？

Kara sits down.
卡拉坐了下來。

Kara: Do you see this icon here?
有沒有看到這個小圖示？

Ted: What's an "icon"?
什麼是「圖示」？

Kara: You don't know what an icon is? You sure don't know much about computers.
你不知道什麼是小圖示嗎？你真的不太懂電腦。

Chapter
1
Chapter
2
Chapter
3
Chapter
4
Chapter
5
Chapter
6
Chapter
7
Chapter
8
Chapter
9
Chapter
10

Ted: I'm a tree planter. I know a lot about trees, rabbits, and bears.

我是種樹的，說到樹木、兔子、熊，我就很熟啊。

Kara: An icon is a symbol. Do you see the icon that I'm pointing at?

小圖示是一種符號。你有沒有看到我現在指的這個圖示？

Ted: Yes.

有。

Kara: This is the icon that you click on to send an email.

按一下這個圖示，你就可以發電子郵件。

Ted: Okay. I'm glad that I'm finally going to learn how to send email.

好的，我好高興終於可以學怎麼發電子郵件了。

Kara: Ted, it would help if you would pay attention.

泰德，如果你專心一點兒會比較好。

Ted: I have a question. What does "email" stand for?

我有一個問題，「email」是什麼意思？

Kara: "Email" is short for "electroni mail".

「Email」就是「electroni mail（電子郵件）」的簡稱。

Ted: I see.

我懂了。

Kara: Now, pay attention.

現在，注意聽。

Ted: Sorry, Kara.

抱歉，卡拉。

Kara: In order to send an email, you must first click on this icon.

要發電子郵件，你必須先按一下這個小圖示。

Ted: How do I do that?

我該怎麼做？

Kara: You use the mouse.

用滑鼠去按。

Ted: A mouse? Where? I'll step on it.

老鼠？在哪裡？我來踩死它。

Kara: Ted.

泰德。

Chapter
1

Chapter
2

Chapter
3

Chapter
4

Chapter
5

Chapter
6

Chapter
7

Chapter
8

Chapter
9

Chapter
10

Ted: Don't worry, Kara. I'll save you. Where did you see the mouse?

別怕，卡拉，我來救妳，老鼠在哪裡？

Kara: Ted!

泰德！

Ted: Yes?

怎麼了？

Kara: This thing lying on the desk is called a "mouse". It's hooked up to the computer.

這個放在桌上，和電腦連在一起的東西，就叫做「滑鼠」。

Ted: This piece of computer equipment is the mouse?

這個電腦設備就叫滑鼠？

Kara: Yes.

沒錯。

Ted: Oh. Sorry.

喔，對不起。

Kara: I can't believe how little you know about computers.

我真不敢相信你對電腦的常識怎麼這麼少。

Questions 習題

_____1. Where does Ted work?

A) In the forest.

B) In the computer tower.

C) At a desk.

D) Ted does not work.

_____2. What does Ted want to learn about?

A) He wants to learn about Kara.

B) He wants to learn how to send an email.

C) He wants to learn about trees, rabbits, and bears.

D) He does not want to learn anything.

_____3. What does email stand for?

A) Empty mail.

B) Enough mail.

C) Elf mail.

D) Electroni mail.

_____4. Who is Ted talking to?

A) The computer

B) Kara

C) The mouse

D) Trees, rabbits, and bears.

Answers 解答

__A__ 1.　**泰德在哪裡工作？**

    A）在森林裡。

    B）在電腦直立主機。

    C）在桌上。

    D）泰德沒有在工作。

__B__ 2.　**泰德想學什麼？**

    A）他想要學有關卡拉的事。

    B）他想要學如何寄電子郵件。

    C）他想要學有關樹、兔子和熊的事。

    D）他不想要學任何東西。

__D__ 3.　**email是什麼意思？**

    A）空的郵件。

    B）足夠的郵件。

    C）精靈郵件。

    D）電子郵件。

__B__ 4.　**泰德在和誰說話？**

    A）電腦

    B）卡拉

    C）滑鼠

    D）樹、兔子和熊。

Vocabulary 字彙通

the computer tower	n.	電腦直立主機
monitor	n.	視器，電腦螢幕
icon	n.	圖示
mouse	n.	滑鼠
hook up	v.	連結，鉤在一起

Addresses
門牌號碼？郵件地址？

Ted is sitting in front of the computer in Kara's house. Kara walks by and looks in.
泰德坐在卡拉屋內的電腦前。卡拉經過那裡，往裡面看。

👤 Ted泰德　　👤 Kara卡拉

Ted: Kara, come here.
卡拉，來一下。

Kara: What are you doing, Ted?
你在做什麼呀，泰德？

Ted: I'm getting ready to send an email. I need your help again.
我準備好要發電子郵件了，再幫我一下。

Kara: We didn't do so well last time we tried this.
我們上次試過，好像不怎麼順利。

Ted: I know but I'm ready to try again. Will you please help me?

我知道，但我現在準備好要再試看看，幫幫我，好嗎？

Kara: All right. Do you see this icon that says "create mail"?

好吧。你有沒有看到這個圖示，上面寫著「新增郵件」？

Ted: Yes.

有啊。

Kara: Click on it.

按一下。

Ted: Okay.

好的。

Kara: Do you see how a new box has opened?

有沒有看到新開一個視窗？

Ted: Yes.

有。

Kara: Do you see where that little thing is flashing?

有沒有看到那個在閃 的小東西？

Ted: What little thing?
什麼小東西？

Kara: That's called the "cursor". Don't ask me why it is called a cursor. It just is.
那個叫「游標」。不要問我它為什麼叫游標，游標就是游標。

Ted: Right.
好吧。

Kara: The cursor is flashing in the space that has the word "to" written in it.
游標閃動的位置，就是要寫「收信者」的地方。

Ted: As in, "to Fred".
譬如在裡面打「弗列德」。

Kara: Right.
沒錯。

Ted: As in, who I am sending the email to.
就是在這裡輸入我要寄信的對象。

Kara: That's right, Ted. That is where you are going to type your address.
沒錯，泰德。你要在那裡輸入你的地址。

Ted: If I wanted to type something in a

different space, I move the cursor, right?
如果我想要在不同的地方打字，就要移動游標？

Kara: Exactly.
完全正確。

Ted: How do you do that?
要怎麼做呢？

Kara: By using your mouse.
用滑鼠。

Ted: Okay. I will move it to where it says "subject".
好，我要把它移到「主旨」那裡。

> Ted moves the mouse around on the desk.
> 泰德在桌上移動滑鼠。

Kara: Now, you can type in what your email is about.
你現在可以輸入你的郵件主題。

Ted: So this is where I type in the subject of my email.
所以我要在這裡輸入郵件主旨。

Kara: That's what I said, Ted.
我就是這個意思，泰德。

Chapter 1
Chapter 2
Chapter 3
Chapter 4
Chapter 5
Chapter 6
Chapter 7
Chapter 8
Chapter 9
Chapter 10

Ted: I don't know what to put as my subject.
我不知道主旨要寫什麼。

Kara: Who are you emailing?
你要寄電子郵件給誰？

Ted: My mom.
我媽。

Kara: Why do you want to email her?
你為什麼要寫信給她？

Ted: I wanted to say hi to her.
想和她打個招呼。

Kara: Why don't you put something like that? Write "hi" or "hi, mom" or "from Ted".
那你要不要這樣寫：「嗨」、「嗨，媽咪」或「泰德的來信」？

Ted: Okay. I am typing "from Ted". Now what?
好吧，我就寫「泰德的來信」。然後呢？

Kara: You had better put in your mother's address.
你最好輸入你媽媽的地址。

Ted: Good idea. Number four, seventeen

Pennycook Street, Vancouver, Canada.
好主意。加拿大，溫哥華市，潘尼寇克17街4號。

Kara: Ted? What are you doing?
泰德，你在做什麼啊？

Ted: You told me to type my mom' address. That's my mom's address.
妳要我輸入我媽的地址，這是她的地址呀。

Kara: Not her street address, Ted! Not her mailing address!
不是她的門牌號碼，泰德！不是她的郵寄地址啦！

Ted: Well, what then? You said type in her address.
不然要輸入什麼？是妳説要輸入她的地址的啊。

Kara: Her email address, Ted. You're sending her an email.
泰德，我是説她的電子郵件地址，你要寄的是電子郵件。

Ted: So?
然後呢？

Kara: You send email to an email address.
電子郵件要寄到電子郵件地址。

Chapter
1
Chapter
2
Chapter
3
Chapter
4
Chapter
5
Chapter
6
Chapter
7
Chapter
8
Chapter
9
Chapter
10

Ted: Oh. Well, isn't that interesting. I don't even know her email address.

哦，這下好了，我不知道她的電子郵件地址。

Kara: Oh, Ted.

天哪，泰德。

Ted: In fact, I don't even know if she has an email address.

老實說，我甚至不知道她有沒有電子郵件地址。

Kara: You're impossible.

你真的很討厭。

Kara leaves.

卡拉走了。

Ted: I'm not even sure if she owns a computer. Isn't that funny, Kara? Kara?

我甚至還不知道她有沒有電腦。這很有趣吧，卡拉？
妳人呢？

Kara: *(yelling)* Good bye Ted.

（大吼）再見，泰德！

Ted: Where are you going? Aren't you going to help me any more?

妳要去哪裡？妳不教我了嗎？

Questions 習題

___1. What does Ted type in the subject area?

A) Hi

B) Hi Mom

C) From Ted

D) Hi Mom from Ted

___2. What street does Ted's mother live on?

A) Vancouver Street

B) Canada Street

C) Pennycook Street

D) Seventeen Street

___3. Why doesn't Ted send an email to his mother?

A) He doesn't know her email address.

B) He doesn't have a computer.

C) Kara won't help him.

D) He doesn't like his mother.

___4. Does Ted's mother have a computer?

A) He does not know.

B) She does not know.

C) She has two.

D) She doesn't use it.

Answers 解答

__C__ 1. 泰德在主旨欄寫了什麼？

A）嗨

B）嗨，媽咪

C）泰德的來信

D）嗨，媽咪—泰德的來信

__C__ 2. 泰德的媽媽住在哪條街？

A）溫哥華街

B）加拿大街

C）潘尼庫克街

D）第十七街

__A__ 3. 泰德為什麼不發電子郵件給他媽媽？

A）他不知道他媽媽的電子郵件地址。

B）他沒有電腦。

C）卡拉不想幫他。

D）他不喜歡他媽媽。

__A__ 4. 泰德的媽媽有電腦嗎？

A）他不知道。

B）她不知道。

C）她有兩台。

D）她沒有用它。

Vocabulary 字彙通

create mail		新增郵件
flash	v.	閃爍
cursor	n.	游標

Unit 3

A New Hobby
一個新嗜好

Anne is sitting on a bench outside. She has a laptop with her. Ted sits down beside her.

安妮坐在戶外的長椅子上，身上帶著筆記型電腦，泰德在她旁邊坐了下來。

 Anne安妮 　　 Ted泰德

Anne: How are you today, Ted?
你今天還好嗎，泰德？

Ted: I'm good. How are you?
好啊，妳呢？

Anne: I'm very good. It's a beautiful day. The sun is shining.
很好啊，今天天氣很好，陽光普照。

Ted: What is new, Anne?
有什麼新鮮事嗎，安妮？

Anne: I'm learning a new hobby.
我在學一樣新玩意。

Ted: Oh? What hobby are you learning?
哦？妳在學什麼玩意？

Anne: I'm learning how to sky dive.
我在學跳傘。

Ted: Are you serious?
你是說真的？

Anne: Yes, I am. It's fun. Have you ever tried it?
是真的，很好玩呢。你有沒有玩過？

Ted: No. You're talking about jumping out of a plane that's up in the air.
沒有。妳是說在半空中，從飛機上跳下來嗎？

Anne: Yes, Ted. It's not much fun to jump out of a plane when it's on the ground.
是啊，泰德。在陸地上從飛機裡跳下來，有什麼好玩的。

Ted: Well, I'm afraid of heights so I would never try it.
喔，我怕高，永遠不可能去玩那個的。

Anne: What's new with you, Ted?
泰德，那你有什麼新鮮事呢？

Chapter 1

Chapter 2

Chapter 3

Chapter 4

Chapter 5

Chapter 6

Chapter 7

Chapter 8

Chapter 9

Chapter 10

Ted: I'm learning a new hobby as well.
我也在學一種新玩意。

Anne: What new hobby have you taken up?
你在學什麼新玩意？

Ted: I'm learning how to email people.
我在學怎麼發電子郵件給別人。

Anne: Are you having fun?
好玩嗎？

Ted: Yes and no. Kara has been helping me. I think that she has lost patience with me.
一半一半。本來卡拉在教我，但我想她已經沒耐心了。

Anne: That's odd. Kara is normally a very patient person.
那就奇怪了，卡拉通常是個很有耐心的人。

Ted: It went well when she helped me. Now it's not going well because I'm on my own.
她教我的時候都好好的，現在我自己弄，進行得不是很順利。

Anne: Well, maybe I can help you. I was going

to check my emails anyway.
好吧，也許我可以幫你，反正我也要收信。

Ted: How nice! Will you check them while I'm here with you?
太好了！妳可不可以趁我在這裡的時候收信？

Anne: Sure, Ted.
當然可以，泰德。

Ted: That way I can ask questions.
這樣我就可以問妳問題了。

Anne: Sure. Let me just get into my email account.
好啊，我要先進入我的電子郵件帳號。

Anne flips open the laptop.
安妮打開筆記型電腦。

Ted: That's where you send and receive emails?
妳在這裡收發電子郵件？

Anne: Yes. It'll just take a second. Here we are. Can you see?
是的，一下就好。就是這裡，看到了嗎？

Chapter
1

Chapter
2

Chapter
3

Chapter
4

Chapter
5

Chapter
6

Chapter
7

Chapter
8

Chapter
9

Chapter
10

Ted: Yes.
看到了。

Anne: So what questions do you have?
好啦，你有什麼問題？

Ted: You type in the email address there and the subject there, right?
妳在這裡輸入郵件地址，在那裡輸入主旨，對吧？

Anne: Right.
是的。

Ted: After you have typed your message in this big space, you just hit send, right?
在這個大空格裡輸入內容後，妳就按傳送，對不對？

Anne: That's right.
沒錯。

Ted: Is that everything I need to know about sending email?
我只要學會這些，就可以發電子郵件了嗎？

Anne: Those are the basics. That's all you need to concern yourself with right now.
那些是基本常識。你現階段只要擔心那些就夠用了。

Ted: Can you tell me about receiving email?
妳可不可以教我怎麼收電子郵件？

Anne: Emails that get sent to you go directly into your inbox.
寄給你的信件會直接跑到你的收件匣裡。

Ted: Okay.
喔。

Anne: You click on the email that you want to read and it will open up.
想看哪封信就在上面點一下，就可以開啟了。

Ted: Okay.
好的。

Anne: Once it's open, you can read it.
郵件一打開，你就可以看了。

Ted: Okay.
了解。

Anne: You haven't received an email yet, have you, Ted?
你還沒收過信是不是，泰德？

Ted: No, I haven't.
還沒。

Chapter
1
Chapter
2
Chapter
3
Chapter
4
Chapter
5
Chapter
6
Chapter
7
Chapter
8
Chapter
9
Chapter
10

Anne: Let's see if I have received any email. I'll show you what I am talking about.
讓我看看我有沒有信進來。我就可以讓你看看我剛說的意思了。

Ted: That would be very nice of you.
妳真好。

Anne: Oh, look, Ted. I have an email from Kara.
你看，泰德，我收到一封卡拉的信。

Ted: What does it say?
裡面寫了什麼？

Anne: Why don't you open it up and read it to me?
你要不要把它打開，讀給我聽？

Ted: All right. It says, "Hi, Anne. I've been helping Ted learn how to use email."
好。它說：「嗨，安妮，我最近在教泰德怎麼用電子郵件」。

Anne: She's talking about you, Ted! What else does it say?
她在說你耶，泰德！還有呢？

Chapter
1

Chapter
2

Chapter
3

Chapter
4

Chapter
5

Chapter
6

Chapter
7

Chapter
8

Chapter
9

Chapter
10

Ted: It says "He's such a pain. He'll probably come and ask you for help, too."
它説：「他真是一個讓人頭痛的傢伙，他可能也會找妳幫忙」。

Anne: Go on. What does the rest say?
繼續呀，她還説了什麼？

Ted: I don't want to tell you.
我不想告訴妳。

Anne: I'll read it myself. It says "Don't do it! He'll drive you crazy."
那我自己讀。它説：「不要教他！他會讓妳抓狂」。

Ted: So. Do you still want to help me learn how to use email?
這下子，妳還要教我怎麼用電子郵件嗎？

____1. What is the weather like?

A) It is cloudy day.

B) It is a rainy day.

C) It is a cold day.

D) The sun is shining.

____2. What is Anne's hobby?

A) Sky diving

B) Learning how to email

C) Helping Ted

D) Talking to Kara

____3. What is Ted's hobby?

A) Sky diving

B) Learning how to email

C) Helping Anne

D) Talking to Kara

____4. Why does Anne jump out of a plane?

A) It is hard.

B) It is fun.

C) She is crazy.

D) She is bored.

Answers 解答

 D 1. **天氣如何？**

A）陰天。

B）雨天。

C）涼爽的天氣。

D）陽光普照。

 A 2. **安妮的興趣是什麼？**

A）跳傘

B）學習如何寄電子郵件

C）幫助泰德

D）跟卡拉説話

 B 3. **泰德的興趣是什麼？**

A）跳傘

B）學習如何寄電子郵件

C）幫助安妮

D）跟卡拉説話

 B 4. **安妮為什麼從飛機上跳下來？**

A）它很難。

B）它很有趣。

C）她瘋了。

D）她覺得無趣。

Vocabulary 字彙通

laptop	n.	手提式個人電腦
hobby	n.	興趣，嗜好
flip	v.	輕彈
inbox	n.	收件匣
drive sb crazy		讓某人抓狂

Chapter

2

Getting Started

開始了

Better to Give Than Receive
寄信總比收信好

Ted is working on a computer.
泰德正在打電腦。

👤 Ted泰德　　👤 Anne安妮

Ted: Anne! Come see!
安妮！快來看！

Anne: What, Ted?
怎麼啦，泰德？

Ted: I just emailed Kara.
我剛剛發了信給卡拉。

Anne: Well done, Ted. Show me what you did.
太好了，泰德。讓我看你怎麼弄的。

Ted: I turned on the computer.
先開機。

Anne: And then?
然後呢？

Ted: I waited for it to warm up. Then I clicked on the icon to get into my email account.
我等它暖機後，就按這個小圖示，來進入我的電子郵件帳號。

Anne: Go on.
繼續。

Ted: I clicked on "new message" and I typed in Kara's address where it's supposed to go.
我按一下「新郵件」，然後在正確位置輸入卡拉的地址。

Anne: Ted?
泰德？

Ted: Don't worry. I didn't type in her street address or mailing address.
放心，我沒有輸入她的門牌號碼或郵寄地址。

Anne: Oh, good.
哦，還好。

Chapter 1
Chapter 2
Chapter 3
Chapter 4
Chapter 5
Chapter 6
Chapter 7
Chapter 8
Chapter 9
Chapter 10

Ted: And in the space that says "subject" I typed what my email is about.
接著在「主旨」的地方，輸入郵件的主題。

Anne: Sounds good so far.
目前聽起來還不錯。

Ted: And then I typed my message to her in the big space and then I hit "send".
然後在大空格裡輸入內容，再按「傳送」。

Anne: Good job, Ted.
好極了，泰德。

Ted: Thank you. Does it sound like I did everything right?
謝謝，這樣聽起來，我是不是都做對了？

Anne: It sounds like it.
應該是。

Ted: So now what do I do?
那現在怎麼辦？

Anne: Now you wait and see if she emails you back.
現在你等看看她有沒有回信給你。

Ted: How do I know that it really went through?
我怎麼知道信寄出去了沒有？

Anne: Do you see where it says "outbox"?
你有沒有看到「寄件匣」？

Ted: Yes.
有。

Anne: The outbox is where emails sit until they get sent or delivered.
還沒寄或還沒傳送的信，都會放在寄件匣裡。

Ted: Okay.
了解。

Anne: Open the outbox by clicking on it.
按一下，打開寄件匣。

Ted: Okay. There's nothing in it.
好的，裡面沒有東西。

Anne: That means that your email has been sent. There's also another way to check.
那就表示你的電子郵件已經寄出去了。還有另一個方法可以檢查。

Chapter 1
Chapter 2
Chapter 3
Chapter 4
Chapter 5
Chapter 6
Chapter 7
Chapter 8
Chapter 9
Chapter 10

Ted: What is it?

什麼方法？

Anne: You can look in the folder called "sent items".

看看「寄件備份」資料夾。

Ted: There it is. I'll click on it to see what is inside.

在那裡，我按一下，看看裡面有什麼。

Anne: And?

有東西嗎？

Ted: I can see a whole list of emails that I have sent. It tells me who I sent each one to.

所有我曾寄的電子郵件都在裡面，還顯示了郵件寄給了誰。

Anne: Can you see the email that you just sent to Kara?

有沒有看到你剛寄給卡拉的信？

Ted: Yes. It's right at the bottom. Well, that's good to know.

有，就在最下面。嗯，知道寄出去了，真好。

Anne: Close out the "sent items" folder.
關上「寄件備份」資料夾。

Ted: Okay.
好的。

Anne: Is there anything in your inbox?
收件匣裡有沒有信？

Ted: Yes! There's an email from Kara.
有！一封卡拉的信。

Ted doesn't open it. Anne is confused.
泰德沒把信打開，安妮覺得很奇怪。

Anne: Aren't you going to open it? Don't you want to see what she sent you?
你不打開嗎？你不想看她寫了什麼給你嗎？

Ted: I'm scared.
我怕。

Anne: What are you scared of?
有什麼好怕的？

Ted: I'm scared to see what she wrote me.
怕看見信的內容。

Chapter 1

Chapter 2

Chapter 3

Chapter 4

Chapter 5

Chapter 6

Chapter 7

Chapter 8

Chapter 9

Chapter 10

Anne: Why?
為什麼？

Ted: Maybe she's probably still mad at me. I was a very difficult student.
也許她還是很生氣，我是一個很難搞的學生。

Anne: Why don't you let me open it? I will tell you what it says.
何不讓我幫你看？我來告訴你信的內容。

Ted: Okay.
好啊。

Anne: Oh, this is very funny.
哦，好好笑喔。

Ted: What? What is it?
什麼？信裡說了什麼？

Anne: This is very funny indeed.
真的好好笑喔。

Ted: What? What did she write?
什麼啦？她寫了什麼？

Anne: She didn't write anything. She sent a picture.
她什麼都沒寫，她寄了一張照片。

Ted: A picture? Of what?
一張照片？什麼照片？

Anne: She sent a picture of herself. She is standing on top of a chair.
她寄了一張自己的照片，她站在椅子上。

Ted: What? Why would she do that?
什麼？她為什麼要那樣做？

Anne: She's pointing at the floor and screaming.
她指著地板，一直尖叫著。

Ted: Why would she send a picture of herself doing that?
她為什麼寄一張這樣的照片呢？

Anne: Because she's scared of a mouse. The computer mouse is under her chair.
因為她怕老鼠。電腦滑鼠在她的椅子下。

Ted: Boy, she really is mad at me.
天哪，她真的很氣我。

Chapter 1

Chapter 2

Chapter 3

Chapter 4

Chapter 5

Chapter 6

Chapter 7

Chapter 8

Chapter 9

Chapter 10

____1. Why is Ted excited?

A) He just sent his first email.

B) He just met Anne for the first time.

C) There is a mouse under his chair.

D) He is scared.

____2. Why is Kara screaming in the picture?

A) Because Ted just sent his first email.

B) Because Ted just met Anne for the first time.

C) Because there is a mouse under her chair.

D) Because Ted is excited.

____3. Who is helping Ted with his email?

A) No one is helping Ted.

B) Kara is helping Ted.

C) Pat is helping Ted.

D) Anne is helping Ted.

____4. What is Ted scared of?

A) He is scared of what Kara will make him wear.

B) He is scared of what Kara will say to him.

C) He is scared of what Kara will do to him.

D) He is scared to see what Kara wrote to him.

Answers 解答

A 1. **為什麼泰德很興奮？**

　　A）他剛剛寄出了第一封電子郵件。

　　B）他第一次遇見安妮。

　　C）有一個滑鼠在他的椅子上。

　　D）他害怕。

C 2. **為何卡拉在照片裡尖叫？**

　　A）因為泰德剛剛寄出了他的第一封電子郵件。

　　B）因為泰德第一次遇見安妮。

　　C）因為有一個滑鼠在他的椅子上。

　　D）因為泰德很興奮。

D 3. **誰在教泰德電子郵件？**

　　A）沒有人在教泰德。

　　B）卡拉在教泰德。

　　C）派得在教泰德。

　　D）安妮在教泰德。

<u>D</u> 4. 泰德怕什麼？

    A）他害怕卡拉要他做的打扮。

    B）他害怕卡拉要告訴他的事。

    C）他害怕卡拉要對他做的事。

    D）他害怕看到卡拉寫給他的內容。

Vocabulary 字彙通

new message	n.	新郵件
subject	n.	主旨
send	v.	傳送
outbox	n.	寄件匣
sent items	n.	寄件備份

Chapter
1

Chapter
2

Chapter
3

Chapter
4

Chapter
5

Chapter
6

Chapter
7

Chapter
8

Chapter
9

Chapter
10

Unit 2 — Too Much 太多了

Anne is sitting on a bench. Kara comes and sits down beside her.
安妮坐在長凳子上，卡拉走過來，坐在她旁邊。

Kara卡拉　　　　Anne安妮　　　　Ted泰德

Kara: Hello, Anne. How are you?
哈囉，安妮，妳好嗎？

Anne: Oh, hello, Kara. I'm good. How are you?
哦，哈囉，卡拉，我還好。妳呢？

Kara: Good. It's a beautiful day. The sun is shining. Are you sure that you are okay?
還不錯。天氣真好，太陽都出來了。妳真的還好嗎？

Anne: Why do you ask?
妳為什麼這樣問？

Kara: You look angry.

妳看起來很生氣。

Anne: No, I'm not angry. I'm squinting. The sun is too bright.
我不是在生氣，我只是在瞇著眼睛，太陽太亮了。

Kara: Here. Put on my sunglasses. Maybe that will help.
拿去，戴上我的太陽眼鏡，這樣可能會好一點。

Anne: Thank you, Kara. What's new?
謝啦，卡拉。最近有什麼事嗎？

Kara: I'll tell you what's new. I get emails from Ted all the time. At least five a day.
我告訴妳最近有什麼事。我一直收到泰德的電子郵件，每天至少五封。

Anne: That's a lot of email.
那還真多呢。

Kara: It sure is. In fact, it's too much.
是很多。事實上，根本就太多了。

Anne: I would say so.
我也這麼覺得。

Kara: Doesn't he have a job to go to?
他沒有事情好做嗎？

Anne: He's a tree planter.

他是個種樹的。

Kara: Right. And what's new with you, Anne?

是啊。安妮，那妳最近有什麼事嗎？

Anne: I'll tell you what's new with me. Ted is always asking me to help him with email.

我告訴你最近有什麼事。泰德一直要我幫他弄電子郵件。

Kara: Poor you.

妳真慘。

Anne: Everyday he asks me to help him. I think that he's asking too much.

他每天都要我幫他，我覺得他問得太多了。

Kara: Why do you think he needs so much help?

妳覺得他為什麼需要這麼多幫忙？

Anne: I don't know. Why do you think that he sends you so many emails?

我也不知道。妳覺得他為什麼寄那麼多電子郵件給妳？

Kara: I have no idea.

我也搞不清楚。

Chapter 1

Chapter 2

Chapter 3

Chapter 4

Chapter 5

Chapter 6

Chapter 7

Chapter 8

Chapter 9

Chapter 10

Anne: Well, we're going to get a chance to ask him because he is walking over right now.
好了,他正好走過來,我們有機會可以問問他了。

Kara: Is he? I'm leaving now. Bye,
真的嗎?我得走了,拜拜。

Anne: Bye, Kara.
拜拜,卡拉。

Kara leaves just as Ted is walking up.
卡拉走出去,剛好泰德走進來。

Anne: Hi, Ted.
嗨,泰德。

Ted: That was Kara, wasn't it? Where's she going?
那不是卡拉嗎?她要去哪裡?

Anne: She had to go to the washroom.
她要去廁所。

Ted: Oh. What were you two doing?
喔,妳們兩個剛剛在做什麼?

Anne: We were just talking about you.
我們在説你。

Ted: You were? What were you saying about me?
是嗎？妳們在説我什麼？

Anne: Kara was saying that you email her too much.
卡拉説你寄太多信給她了。

Ted: Oh? What about you, Anne? What were you saying about me?
哦？那妳呢，安妮？妳説了我什麼？

Anne: I was just telling Kara that you ask for help too much.
我告訴卡拉説你要我幫太多忙了。

Ted: Really?
真的嗎？

Anne: Yes. You ask me to help you with your emails everyday.
嗯，你每天都要我幫你弄電子郵件。

Ted: I do? I didn't realize that I was asking

Chapter 1

Chapter 2

Chapter 3

Chapter 4

Chapter 5

Chapter 6

Chapter 7

Chapter 8

Chapter 9

Chapter 10

that often.
是嗎？我都不知道我那麼常問妳。

Anne: You are, Ted. You send Kara at least five emails a day.
你常常問，泰德。你每天至少寄五封信給卡拉。

Ted: I do? I had no idea that I was sending her that many emails.
真的？我都不曉得自己每天寄那麼多信給她。

Anne: You are, Ted.
你的確這樣做了，泰德。

Ted: I'm sorry. I'm sorry that I'm asking you for too much help.
真對不起。不好意思，我每天問妳太多問題了。

Anne: It's okay.
沒關係啦。

Ted: Well, that's good.
那就好。

Anne: So what's new with you, Ted?
最近有什麼事嗎，泰德？

Ted: Well, I have a problem.
嗯，有個麻煩。

Anne: You do?
哦？

Ted: Yes. I was going to ask you about it, Anne.
嗯，我本來要問妳的呢，安妮。

Anne: Well, I will gladly help you. That's what friends are for.
我很樂意幫忙，這就是朋友啊。

Ted: Thank you. That's very nice of you. I was also going to email Kara about it.
謝謝，妳真好。我也正想發電子郵件給卡拉。

Anne: I'm sure she would want to know if you had a problem.
我想你如果有麻煩，她一定也很想知道。

Ted: You think so?
妳確定嗎？

Anne: I'm sure that she'd want to help. That's what friends are for. What is it?
我確定她會幫忙，這樣才是朋友啊。你有什麼問題？

Ted: I have too many emails in my inbox. It's too much. How do I get rid of them?

Chapter
1

Chapter
2

Chapter
3

Chapter
4

Chapter
5

Chapter
6

Chapter
7

Chapter
8

Chapter
9

Chapter
10

我收件匣裡的信太多了，多到不行。我要怎麼把它們弄掉？

Anne: I'm out of here.
我要走了。

Anne leaves.
安妮正要離開。

Ted: Anne? Why are you leaving? Aren't you going to help me?
安妮？妳為什麼要走呢？妳不幫我了嗎？

___1. Why is Anne squinting?

A) She has sun glasses on.

B) She is angry.

C) She is not okay.

D) The sun is too bright.

___2. How many emails does Kara get from Ted each day?

A) At least ten

B) At least five

C) At least six

D) At least nine

___3. Who does Ted ask too much for help?

A) Kara

B) His mother

C) Anne

D) The tutor

___4. Who thinks that it is a beautiful day?

A) Kara

B) Kara and Anne

C) Kara, Anne, and Ted

D) None of the above

 D 1.　**安妮為什麼瞇著眼睛？**

　　A）她戴著太陽眼鏡。

　　B）她在生氣。

　　C）她不太好。

　　D）太陽太亮了。

 B 2.　**卡拉每天收到幾 泰德的信？**

　　A）至少十

　　B）至少五

　　C）至少六

　　D）至少九

 C 3.　**泰德要誰幫太多的忙？**

　　A）卡拉

　　B）他媽媽

　　C）安妮

　　D）家庭教師

 A 4.　**誰覺得今天天氣很好？**

　　A）卡拉

　　B）卡拉和安妮

　　C）卡拉、安妮和泰德

　　D）以上皆非

Vocabulary 字彙通

　　squint　　　　　　　　v.　　　瞇著眼看

Chapter
1

Chapter
2

Chapter
3

Chapter
4

Chapter
5

Chapter
6

Chapter
7

Chapter
8

Chapter
9

Chapter
10

Unit
3

All Gone

全部刪除

Ted and Bill are sitting together in front of the computer. Bill is eating his lunch.

泰德和比爾一起坐在電腦前，比爾正在吃午餐。

 Ted泰德　　　Bill比爾

Ted: Thank you for coming, Bill.
比爾，謝謝你過來。

Bill: I'm happy to be able to help.
我很樂意幫你。

Ted: That's good. My other friends have given up on me.
那就好，我的其他朋友都放棄我了。

Bill: I enjoy teaching people. That's why I tutor people.
我很喜歡教人家東西，所以才會當家教。

Ted: Your lunch smells good.
你的午餐聞起來好香哦。

Bill: I'm sorry that I am eating in front of you. I haven't had a chance to eat yet.
不好意思，在你面前用餐。我還沒時間吃飯。

Ted: Don't worry about it. Please go ahead.
沒關係，你慢用。

Bill: Thank you.
謝謝。

Ted: I have lots of emails in my inbox. I don't know how to get rid of them.
我的收件匣裡有一大堆信，不知道該怎麼把它們弄掉。

Bill: You need to delete them.
你必須把它們刪除。

Ted: How do I do that?
要怎麼做呢？

Bill: Go into your email account. Now go into your inbox. Click on one email that you want to delete. Do you see the button at the top of your screen that is called "delete"?
進入你的郵件帳號，到收件匣裡，點選你要刪除的郵件。有沒有看到螢幕上面那個「刪除」按鈕？

Ted: Yes.
有。

Bill: Click on it.
按下去。

Ted: That message is all gone!
那封信不見了！

Bill: When you want to delete an email, highlight it and then click "delete".
當你要刪除一封信時，先把它反白，再按「刪除」。

Ted: Where does it go?
它到哪裡去了呢？

Bill: It goes into your trash.
到你的垃圾桶裡去了。

Ted looks confused.
泰德看起來一臉迷惑。

Ted: Under the sink? How could it possibly get in there?
在水槽下面？它怎麼可能去那裡呢？

Chapter
1

Chapter
2

Chapter
3

Chapter
4

Chapter
5

Chapter
6

Chapter
7

Chapter
8

Chapter
9

Chapter
10

Bill: Not the trash in your kitchen Ted. It goes into the folder called "trash".

不是你廚房裡的垃圾桶，泰德，它去了一個叫做「垃圾桶」的資料夾裡。

Ted: What happens when the trash folder is full? How do you empty the trash?

要是垃圾桶資料夾滿了，該怎麼辦？你怎麼清垃圾桶？

Bill: If you right click on the trash folder, a menu will come up.

如果你在垃圾桶資料夾上，按下右鍵，就會出現一個選單。

Ted: I see it.

我看到了。

Bill: In that menu, you will see the words "empty trash".

你會在選單裡看到「清空垃圾桶」這些字。

Ted: Yes.

嗯。

Bill: Right click on those words.

在這些字上按下右鍵。

Ted: Okay. The trash folder is now empty. I like deleting stuff. What else can I delete?
好的，垃圾桶資料夾清空了。我真喜歡刪除東西，還有什麼可以刪的？

Bill: Delete unwanted messages from your "inbox", "trash", and "sent items" folders.
你可以刪除你的「收件匣」、「垃圾桶」和「寄件備份」資料夾裡不要的信件。

Ted: I'll try and delete a message from my "sent items" folder. Select, click, and look!
我來刪刪看「寄件備份」資料夾裡的信。選取，按一下，你看！

Bill: It's all gone. Good job. You seem to understand how to delete things now.
不見了。做得好。你似乎已經知道怎麼刪除信件了。

Ted: Yes, I do.
是的，我知道了。

Bill: Good. Our time is almost over and I have another student to tutor after you.
很好。我們的時間快到了，接下來我還有另一個學生要教。

Chapter 1

Chapter 2

Chapter 3

Chapter 4

Chapter 5

Chapter 6

Chapter 7

Chapter 8

Chapter 9

Chapter 10

Ted: Okay.

好的。

Bill: Did you have any other questions for me today?

今天還有什麼問題要問我嗎？

Ted: Yes. Can I please have some of your lunch? It smells so good.

有。我可不可以嚐嚐你的午餐？好香哦。

___1. Why does Ted need a tutor?

A) He doesn't need a tutor.

B) He needs help in math.

C) He is falling behind.

D) His other friends have given up on him.

___2. Who is tutoring Ted?

A) Kara

B) Bill

C) Anne

D) Kara, Bill, and Anne

___3. Why does Ted what some of Bill's lunch?

A) He doesn't.

B) It smells great.

C) It is Ted's lunch.

D) Ted is a thief.

___4. How does Ted know that Bill has a good lunch?

A) He doesn't.

B) It smells great.

C) It smells horrible.

D) A mouse ate it.

Answers 解答

<u>B</u> 1.　**為什麼泰德需要家教？**

A) 他不需要家庭教師。

B) 他的數學需要幫助。

C) 他落後了。

D) 他的其他朋友已經放棄他了。

<u>B</u> 2.　**誰在教泰德？**

A) 卡拉

B) 比爾

C) 安妮

D) 卡拉、比爾和安妮

<u>B</u> 3.　**為什麼泰德要嚐嚐比爾的午餐？**

A) 他沒有嚐。

B) 它聞起來很香。

C) 它是泰德的午餐。

D) 泰德是小偷。

<u>B</u> 4.　**泰德怎麼知道比爾的午餐很好吃？**

A) 他不知道。

B) 它聞起來很香。

C) 它聞起來很糟。

D) 一隻老鼠吃了它。

Vocabulary 字彙通

tutor	v.	當家庭教師
highlight	v.	強調
folder	n.	資料夾
trash	n.	垃圾桶
empty	v.	倒空

Chapter

3

Making Progress

有進步

Getting Attached
附加檔案

Bill is sitting with Ted in front of the computer.
比爾和泰德坐在電腦前面。

Ted 泰德　　Bill 比爾

Ted: I sure enjoy having you as my tutor, Bill.
比爾，我很喜歡你當我的家教。

Bill: Why, thank you, Ted.
喔，謝謝你，泰德。

Ted: I think that you're a great teacher.
我覺得你是一個很棒的老師。

Bill: And unlike what your friends say, I find you very easy to get along with.
我也覺得你很容易相處，不像你朋友說的那樣。

Ted: Really?
真的嗎？

Bill: I think that you're a good student. You make it very easy to teach.
我覺得你是一個很好的學生，很容易教。

Ted: What a nice compliment. What are we going to talk about today Bill?
好棒的讚美。我們今天要學什麼呢，比爾？

Bill: We're going to talk about attachments.
今天要談怎麼附加東西。

Ted: I'm very attached to my Mom and Dad. I'm quite attached to my pet dog as well.
我很依賴我的父母，也很依戀我心愛的狗狗。

Bill: I don't mean those kinds of attachments.
我不是說那種依附。

Ted: Oh. Do you mean how my legs and arms are attached to my body?
哦。那你指手腳怎麼附在我身上？

Bill: No!
不是！

Ted: Maybe you mean the type of attachments that are removable.
還是說那些可以拿掉的附件？

Chapter 1
Chapter 2
Chapter 3
Chapter 4
Chapter 5
Chapter 6
Chapter 7
Chapter 8
Chapter 9
Chapter 10

Bill: What are you talking about?

你在說什麼呀？

Ted: I have a vacuum cleaner that has different attachments.

我有一個吸塵器，上面有各式各樣的附件。

Bill: What?

什麼呀？

Ted: Yes. When you're done using them, you can take them off.

對啊，當你不用它們的時候，就可以把它們拿掉。

Bill: Ted, I am talking about attaching another file to your email message.

泰德，我是說在你的電子郵件裡，附上另一個檔案。

Ted: Oh! That sounds interesting.

哦，聽起來很有意思。

Bill: Sometimes you want to send something by email like a document or a photo.

有時候你會想要用電子郵件傳送文件或照片之類的東西。

Ted: Okay.

嗯。

Bill: You can attach these things to your email. Let's get started.
你就可以把這些附在電子郵件裡。我們來試試看。

Ted: Okay.
好的。

Bill: Please insert this disk into your computer.
把這張磁片放進電腦裡。

Ted: Sure.
好。

Bill gives a disk to Ted who inserts it into the computer.
比爾給泰德一張磁片，泰德把它放進電腦裡。

Bill: Now prepare a message to me. You remember my email address, don't you?
現在，寫一封信給我，你記得我的電子郵件地址吧？

Ted: Yes. How's this? "Hi, Bill. Thanks for teaching me about attachments."
記得。這麼寫怎麼樣？「嗨，比爾，謝謝你教我附加檔案」。

Bill: Good. Let's say that there's something on this disk that you want to send to me.
可以，假設你要寄這張磁片上的東西給我。

Ted: Okay.

好。

Bill: Hit "attach".

按下「附加」。

Ted: Okay.

好了。

Bill: Now click on "three and a half inch floppy" because that is where your document is.

現在選取「3.5 磁片」，檔案在裡面。

Ted: There's a document named "to Bill". Is that the one you want me to attach?

有一個檔案叫做「給比爾」，那就是你要我附加的檔案嗎？

Bill: Yes.

是的。

Ted: Okay. Now, what do I do?

好了，現在要做什麼？

Bill: Select that file. Hit the attach button. The mail and attachment are ready to send.

選取那個檔案，按一下附加按鈕。信件和檔案都準備好要傳送了。

Ted: What am I sending?

我寄的是什麼？

Bill: It doesn't matter, Ted. This is just an exercise.

那不重要，泰德，這只是練習。

Ted: I want to know what I'm sending.

我想要知道我寄的是什麼。

Bill: Ted, just hit "send".

泰德，只要按「傳送」就好了。

Ted: Not until you tell me what I'm sending.

如果你不告訴我，我就不寄。

Bill: I can't believe how paranoid you are being.

我真不敢相信你這麼疑神疑鬼。

Ted: I'm going to read this attachment that you're making me send to you.

我要看你讓我寄給你的附件。

Bill: If you must.

如果你一定要看的話。

Chapter 1

Chapter 2

Chapter 3

Chapter 4

Chapter 5

Chapter 6

Chapter 7

Chapter 8

Chapter 9

Chapter 10

Ted: It says, "Hi, Ted. If you're reading this, you are very paranoid".

它寫説：「嗨，泰德，如果你正在看，你真是疑神疑鬼」。

Bill: So what do you have to say for yourself?

現在你還有什麼話説？

Ted: Now, I'm embarrassed.

我覺得很不好意思。

Bill: I told you that there was nothing in this attachment to be worried about.

我跟你説過，那個附加檔案裡沒什麼大不了的東西。

Ted: I guess I need to detach myself from being paranoid.

我想我該把身上疑神疑鬼的附件拆掉。

Bill: That's a horrible joke, Ted.

這個笑話太冷了，泰德。

___1. When did Ted feel embarrassed?

A) After he read the attachment

B) After he called Bill a bad name

C) After he asked Bill for some of his lunch.

D) After he mad a horrible joke.

___2. How did Ted attach the document?

A) With a stapler

B) With glue

C) With a hot glue gun

D) By clicking on "attach"

___3. What did Bill say about Ted's friends?

A) He doesn't care about them.

B) He doesn't care what they say.

C) He doesn't care what they think.

D) He doesn't care what they wear.

___4. Who is Ted attached to?

A) His mother

B) His mother, father and pet dog

C) His father

D) His father and Bill and his pet dog

_A_ 1. 泰德何時覺得不好意思？

A）在他讀了附件之後

B）在他叫比爾一個難聽的名字後

C）在他請比爾給他一些午餐後。

D）在他做了一個糟糕的惡作劇後。

_D_ 2. 泰德如何附加檔案？

A）用釘書機

B）用膠水

C）用熱熔膠

D）按「附加」

_C_ 3. 比爾對泰德的朋友有何感覺？

A）他不在乎他們。

B）他不在乎他們説什麼。

C）他不在乎他們怎麼想。

D）他不在乎他們穿什麼。

_B_ 4. 泰德很依賴誰？

A）他的媽媽

B）他的媽媽和爸爸和寵物狗

C）他的爸爸

D）他的爸爸、比爾和他的寵物狗

Vocabulary 字彙通

attachment	n.	附件
attach	v.	附加
vacuum cleaner	n.	吸塵器
three and a half inch floppy		
	n.	3.5磁片
paranoid	adj.	過分猜疑偏執狂的
detach	v.	拆卸，分開

A Quick Reply
速速回覆

Bill and Ted are sitting together in front of the computer.
比爾和泰德一起坐在電腦前。

👤 Bill比爾　　👤 Ted泰德

Bill: Ted, each time I send you an email, you send a new message back to me.
泰德，每次我寄一郵件給你，你都會寄一新郵件回來。

Ted: Of course, I do. Why?
當然啊，怎麼了？

Bill: When you send a new message to me, I can't see what I wrote to you.
當你寄新郵件給我時，我就不曉得我原來那信的內容了。

Ted: So?
要不然呢？

Bill: It'd be best if I could see what I wrote to

you and what you wrote back.
如果我能看見原來的信，也能看見你的回信，就最好了。

Ted: That would be ideal, I guess.
我想那會比較理想。

Bill: Sometimes I can't remember what I sent you.
有時候，我不記得我到底寄了什麼給你。

Ted: I know the feeling.
我知道那種感覺。

Bill: I read your email and wonder what you're talking about.
當我讀你的信時，會不知道你在説些什麼。

Ted: You can't remember your message to me.
你不記得你寫了什麼給我。

Bill: Right.
對啊。

Ted: But what can I do about it?
那要怎麼辦呢？

Bill: You can click on the "reply" button after you have read an email.
你看完信後，可以按「回覆」按鈕。

Chapter
1

Chapter
2

Chapter
3

Chapter
4

Chapter
5

Chapter
6

Chapter
7

Chapter
8

Chapter
9

Chapter
10

Ted: Is that what that's for?
那個按鈕的功能就是這個？

Bill: Don't click on the "new message" button.
不要按「新郵件」的按鈕。

Ted: Okay.
好的。

Bill: You can send email back to the sender.
你可以回信給寄件人。

Ted: Cool.
這很酷呢！

Bill: It will have what they wrote and what you are writing. Try it.
這樣信裡就會有寄件人和你所寫的內容，試試看。

Ted: Okay.
好的。

Bill: Pick an email from your inbox that you haven't read yet.
從收件匣裡選一 你還沒看過的信。

Ted: Okay.
好的。

Bill: Read it and then click on "reply".
看完信後，按「回覆」按鈕。

Ted reads silently.
泰德靜靜地讀信。

Bill: Now you can send your response and it will include what they wrote.
現在，你可以寄出回信，包括原寄件人寫的內容。

Ted: Cool.
酷！

Bill: Two days ago, I sent you an email asking if you were going to the movie.
兩天前，我寫信問你要不要去看電影。

Ted: I emailed you back and said I was.
我回信說好呀。

Bill: Exactly. All your email said was the word "yes".
是呀，你信裡只寫一個字：「要」。

Ted: So?
然後呢？

Chapter
1

Chapter
2

Chapter
3

Chapter
4

Chapter
5

Chapter
6

Chapter
7

Chapter
8

Chapter
9

Chapter
10

Bill: I didn't know which of my emails you were responding to.

我搞不清楚你回的是哪封信。

Ted: Oh.

喔。

Bill: And I couldn't remember what I had asked you.

我也不記得我自己問了你什麼。

Ted: Oh.

喔。

Bill: I get these emails from you and all they say is, "yes" or "no" or "maybe".

你寫給我的信都只說「好」、「不好」或「可能吧」。

Ted: Yes.

對啊。

Bill: I never know what it's about. Now you can click "reply" instead of "new message".

我根本不知道它們在說什麼。現在你可以按「回覆」按鈕，而不要按「新郵件」。

Ted: Right.
好的。

Bill: That way, I can see what my question was and what your answer is.
這樣子的話，我就能看到自己的問題和你的答覆。

Ted: Okay. Then can you reply to my reply?
好的，這樣你能對我的答覆做出回覆嗎？

Bill: I sure can.
當然能。

Ted: And then I can reply to your reply to my reply, right?
這樣我就能回覆你對我的答覆的回覆，對嗎？

Bill: That's right, Ted.
沒錯，泰德。

Ted: And then you can reply to my reply to your reply to my reply.
然後你就能回覆，我回覆你，回覆給我的答覆。

Bill: Now, you're just being silly.
好啦，你又開始傻言傻語了。

Chapter 1
Chapter 2
Chapter 3
Chapter 4
Chapter 5
Chapter 6
Chapter 7
Chapter 8
Chapter 9
Chapter 10

Ted: Do you want to know what my reply to that is?

你想不想知道，我對那個的回覆是什麼？

Bill: No.

不想。

Ted: What about words that rhyme with "reply"? Do you want to know what they are?

和「回覆」押韻的字如何？想不想知道有哪些字？

Bill: No.

不想。

Ted: Come on. There're all kinds of words that rhyme with "reply".

別這樣，好多字都和「回覆」（reply）押韻。

Bill: Ted.

泰德。

Ted: Try, fly, die, pie...

Try（試），fly（飛），die（死），pie（派）……

90

Bill: Ted.
泰德。

Ted: Sigh, lie, my...
Sigh（嘆氣）, lie（說謊）, my（我的）……

Bill stands up.
比爾站了起來。

Bill: I don't have time for this. Ted!
我沒空和你扯這些，泰德！

Ted: What?
什麼？

Bill: Here's a word that rhymes with reply.
我有一個和「回覆」押韻的字。

Ted: Oh, goodie. What is it?
太讚了，是什麼字？

Bill: Bye. Find yourself a new tutor. I've had it.
Bye（再見）! 你換個老師吧，我受夠了。

Ted: Please don't quit on me.
求求你別放棄我。

Chapter 1
Chapter 2
Chapter 3
Chapter 4
Chapter 5
Chapter 6
Chapter 7
Chapter 8
Chapter 9
Chapter 10

Bill: I don't have the patience to keep working with you. Sorry, Ted.

我沒耐心教你了，對不起，泰德。

Bill leaves.
比爾離開了。

Ted: Why? Don't go bye. Bill? Bill? He's gone. Oh, my.

為什麼？別說再見嘛，比爾、比爾？天哪，他真的走了。

___1. Who taught Ted how to reply?

A) Kara

B) Anne

C) Bill

D) Ted's mother

___2. What did Ted do that made Bill quit?

A) He started singing.

B) He started telling jokes.

C) He started hitting Bill.

D) He started rhyming.

___3. Where did Bill go when he left Ted?

A) It doesn't say.

B) To the mall

C) Back to school

D) To call a friend

___4. Why did Bill leave?

A) He quit.

B) He had to go.

C) Ted told him to leave.

D) The sun was in his eyes.

__C__ 1. 誰教泰德如何回信？

    A）卡拉

    B）安妮

    C）比爾

    D）泰德的媽媽

__D__ 2. 泰德做了什麼把比爾給氣跑了？

    A）他開始唱歌。

    B）他開始説笑話。

    C）他開始打比爾。

    D）他開始玩押韻遊戲。

__A__ 3. 比爾離開泰德後，去了哪裡？

    A）沒有説。

    B）去商場

    C）回學校

    D）打電話給一個朋友

__B__ 4. 比爾為何要離開？

    A）他辭職。

    B）他必須要離開。

    C）泰德叫他離開。

    D）陽光刺進他的眼裡。

Vocabulary 字彙通

reply	v.	回覆
new message	n.	新郵件

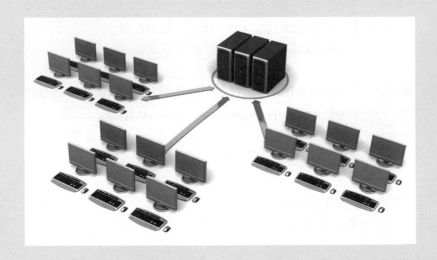

Moving Forward

過去的，就過去了

Anne and Bill are sitting at a table in the cafeteria.
安妮和比爾坐在一家自助餐店裡。

Bill比爾

Anne安妮

Ted泰德

Bill: Ted drives me crazy. I feel bad because I've given up on him, Anne.
泰德把我搞瘋了。我很難過我放棄他了，安妮。

Anne: You shouldn't feel bad, Bill. It's not your fault. Ted is hard to work with.
你不應該難過的，比爾。這不是你的錯。泰德是一個很難搞的人。

Bill: I suppose.
我也這麼覺得。

Anne: Don't worry about Ted. He's fine. He

knows that he can be a pain.
別擔心泰德，他沒事的，他知道自己是個頭痛的傢伙。

Bill: He does?
真的嗎？

Anne: Yes. I think that he enjoys being difficult. He likes to irritate people.
真的，我覺得他為此沾沾自喜。他喜歡把別人惹火。

Bill: You think so?
妳真的這麼認為？

Anne: I do. Please don't worry or feel guilty. It's best if you just try to move forward.
是啊。請別擔心，也不要有罪惡感。重要的是你得讓事情過去。

Bill: It may be hard for me to forget about it right now.
現在要我忘記，有點難。

Anne: Why's that?
為什麼呢？

Bill: Ted is coming over to us right now. I am going to go now, Anne.
泰德現在正朝我們走過來。我得走了，安妮。

Chapter 1
Chapter 2
Chapter 3
Chapter 4
Chapter 5
Chapter 6
Chapter 7
Chapter 8
Chapter 9
Chapter 10

Anne: Okay, Bill.
好的。比爾。

Bill: Say hi to Ted for me.
幫我向泰德問好。

Anne: I will.
我會的。

Bill gets up and leaves just as Ted arrives.
比爾起身離開，剛好泰德走過來。

Ted: Hello, Anne.
哈囉，安妮。

Anne: Hello, Ted.
哈囉，泰德。

Ted: That was Bill, wasn't it? Where's Bill going?
那不是比爾嗎？他要去哪裡？

Anne: He had to use the washroom.
他要去洗手間。

Ted: What were you two talking about?
你們在談什麼啊？

Anne: We were talking about you. We were just saying how difficult you can be.

我們在談你，説你是一個難搞的人。

Ted: Yes, I sure can be.

是啊，我的確是。

Anne: If you know it, why do you do it?

既然你知道，為什麼還要這樣？

Ted: I don't know. I think that maybe I enjoy it a little.

我不曉得，也許我有點喜歡這樣做。

Anne: You enjoy bugging people? Ted, I don't know what to think about you.

你喜歡給人找麻煩？泰德，我真不知道該怎麼想你這個人。

Ted: Oh.

喔。

Anne: Bill doesn't know what to think about you. Kara doesn't either.

比爾不知道該對你有何感想，卡拉也是。

Ted: I see.

我知道。

Chapter 1

Chapter 2

Chapter 3

Chapter 4

Chapter 5

Chapter 6

Chapter 7

Chapter 8

Chapter 9

Chapter 10

Anne: I told Bill that he has to do what Kara and I both did. He has to move forward.

我告訴比爾，他必須和卡拉跟我一樣，讓事情過去。

Ted: I hope that Bill doesn't have any hard feelings. Anne is Bill mad at me?

我希望比爾不會覺得很不舒服。安妮，他很氣我嗎？

Anne: Of course.

當然。

Ted: I hope that he can get over being mad at me.

我希望他不要再生我的氣了。

Anne: I'm sure he will, with time. We talked about him needing to move forward.

我確定他慢慢就會沒事了。我們剛剛也在說，他必須讓事情過去。

Ted: Speaking of moving forward, can you teach me about forwarding email messages?

說到讓事情過去，妳能不能教我怎麼把信件轉寄出去？

Anne: Yes, I can, Ted. First, you must promise not to try and annoy me.

可以啊，泰德。首先，你要保證不把我惹火。

Ted: I promise.
我保證。

Anne: Okay. Good. Now, to forward an email you must go into your inbox.
很好。現在，要轉寄信件，你必須先進到收件匣裡。

Ted flips open a notebook he is carrying.
泰德打開他帶的筆記型電腦。

Ted: Okay.
好了。

Anne: Highlight the email that you wish to forward.
把你要轉寄的信反白。

Ted: Okay.
好了。

Anne: Click on the button that says "forward".
按下「轉寄」按鈕。

Ted: Done.
完成。

Anne: Do you see the message box that has popped up?
你有沒有看到一個對話視窗跳了出來？

Chapter
1

Chapter
2

Chapter
3

Chapter
4

Chapter
5

Chapter
6

Chapter
7

Chapter
8

Chapter
9

Chapter
10

Ted: Yes.
有。

Anne: Type in the email address that you wish to forward that message to.
輸入你要轉寄的郵件地址。

Ted: That's it?
就這樣而已？

Anne: Well, once you hit "send" then yes, that's it.
嗯，按下「傳送」就好了，就是這樣。

Ted: Wow. That was easy.
哇，真簡單。

Anne: Yes, it was.
是很簡單。

Ted: And I didn't even bug you.
而且我也沒找妳麻煩。

Anne: I know. It is hard to believe, isn't it?
是啊，真不可思議，不是嗎？

___1. When did Bill leave?

A) Right after Ted came

B) Right before Ted came

C) When Anne told him to

D) When Anne asked him to

___2. Why did Bill leave?

A) He had to tutor someone.

B) He had to go to the bathroom.

C) His mother was calling him.

D) No reason is given.

___3. What did Bill promise to Anne?

A) He promised not to bug her.

B) He promised to come back.

C) He did not promise her anything.

D) He promised to give her cookies.

Chapter

3

 A 1.　**比爾何時離開？**

A) 在泰德來之後

B) 在泰德來之前

C) 當安妮告訴他

D) 當安妮要求

 D 2.　**比爾為何要離開？**

A) 他必須要去當某人的家庭教師。

B) 他必須要去洗澡。

C) 他媽媽正打電話給他。

D) 沒有給理由。

 C 3.　**比爾向安妮保證什麼？**

A) 他保證不會糾纏她。

B) 他保證會回來。

C) 他沒有向她保證任何事情。

D) 他保證要給她點心。

Vocabulary 字彙通

cafeteria	n.	自助餐館
irritate	v.	激怒
pop up		（突然地）出現

Chapter

4

Improving

改善中

Getting Better
漸入佳境

Kara is sitting on a bench. Bill joins her.
卡拉坐在長凳子上，比爾過來和她坐在一起。

👤 Bill比爾　　👤 Kara卡拉

Bill: The weather is getting better.
天氣逐漸變好了。

Kara: We had some very poor weather for a while.
這個壞天氣已經持續好一陣子了。

Bill: How are you feeling? Anne told me that you had a cold.
妳現在覺得怎麼樣？安妮告訴我妳感冒了。

Kara: I was not feeling well but I am getting better.
之前不太舒服，現在好多了。

Bill: That's good. How's Anne?
那就好。安妮還好嗎？

Kara: Anne was in a car accident.
她出車禍了。

Bill: Oh, no. Is she okay?
喔，天哪，她沒事吧？

Kara: Yes. She is fine.
她沒事。

Bill: What happened?
發生什麼事了？

Kara: She was driving her motorcycle. A car hit her at an intersection with no traffic lights.
她騎摩托車，在一個沒有紅綠燈的路口，被一輛汽車撞到。

Bill: There should be a sign or some traffic lights at every intersection.
每個路口都該有號誌或紅綠燈。

Kara: This intersection has always been very bad in the past.
過去這個路口的狀況一直很糟。

Bill: So Anne is okay? She wasn't hurt?
所以，安妮還好嗎？沒受傷吧？

Chapter
1

Chapter
2

Chapter
3

Chapter
4

Chapter
5

Chapter
6

Chapter
7

Chapter
8

Chapter
9

Chapter
10

Kara: She has a broken wrist. She tells me that her wrist is getting better and better.
她手腕脫臼了。她告訴我，她的手腕逐漸在復原中。

Bill: That's good.
那就好。

Kara: She says that it's healing quickly. Are you still tutoring Ted?
她說復原得很快。你還在教泰德嗎？

Bill: No. At first, I couldn't understand why you and Anne both stopped teaching him.
沒有。起初，我不明白為什麼妳和安妮都不教他了。

Kara: Oh?
哦？

Bill: However, I soon began to understand why. Ted will drive you crazy.
但是，後來我就知道了。泰德他會把人搞瘋。

Kara: He's gotten better.
他現在好多了。

Bill: He has?
是嗎？

Kara: Oh, yes. He used to make me angry in seconds.
沒錯，以前他不到兩秒鐘，就會把我氣死。

> Bill laughs. Kara smiles.
> 比爾大笑，卡拉也笑了笑。

Bill: Really?
真的？

Kara: Yes. Now it takes minutes for me to get angry with him.
真的。現在我大概隔幾分鐘，才會對他發脾氣。

Bill: I guess that's an improvement.
這表示他有改善。

Kara: It is definitely better than it used to be.
絕對是比以前好多了。

Bill: Ted has really improved at using email.
他現在用電子郵件也進步多了。

Kara: Has he?
真的？

Bill: Yes. He has gotten better and better at it.
真的，而且愈來愈好。

Chapter 1
Chapter 2
Chapter 3
Chapter 4
Chapter 5
Chapter 6
Chapter 7
Chapter 8
Chapter 9
Chapter 10

Kara: You're a good teacher.
你真是一個好老師。

Bill: So are you and so is Anne.
妳和安妮也是。

Kara: Ted is lucky to have such good friends. So, tell me. What has he learned?
泰德真幸運，有這麼多好朋友。那你告訴我，他學了些什麼？

Bill: How to send email, how to check messages, delete, reply, and how to attach.
怎麼發電子郵件、如何查看郵件、刪除、回覆，和附加檔案。

Kara: Well, he has definitely gotten better at using his email.
哇，他現在一定很會用電子郵件了。

Bill: Yes.
是啊。

Kara: When I was helping him, we had trouble with email addresses.
當我在教他的時候，連郵件地址都會搞半天。

Bill: I know.
我知道。

Kara: When Anne was helping him, I had trouble with getting five emails a day.
安妮教他的時候，他每天至少發五封信給我。

Bill: I heard about that.
我聽說了。

Kara: It's much better now.
現在好多了。

Bill: Really?
真的嗎？

Kara: Oh, yes. I only get one or two emails a day from him now.
當然，我現在每天只收到他一、兩封信。

____1. Who used to get five emails a day from Ted?
   A) Bill
   B) Anne
   C) Kara
   D) Ted

____2. What happened to Anne?
   A) She went skydiving and broke her wrist.
   B) She was in a car accident and broke her wrist.
   C) She ate a sandwich and broke her wrist.
   D) She emailed Ted and broke her wrist.

____3. Where is Anne?
   A) We do not know.
   B) She is with Bill.
   C) She is with Ted.
   D) She is with Kara.

____4. How did Anne break her wrist?
   A) She was in a car accident.
   B) She was in a plane accident.
   C) She was in a boating accident.
   D) She was in a sports accident.

Answers 解答

<u>C</u> 1. 哪個人以前每天收到五封泰德的信？

A）比爾

B）安妮

C）卡拉

D）泰德

<u>B</u> 2. 安妮怎麼了？

A）她去跳傘，手腕脫臼了。

B）她出車禍，手腕脫臼了。

C）她吃了一個三明治，手腕脫臼了。

D）她寫電子郵件給泰德，手腕脫臼了。

<u>A</u> 3. 安妮在哪裡？

A）我們不知道。

B）她跟比爾在一起。

C）她跟泰德在一起。

D）她跟卡拉在一起。

<u>A</u> 4. 安妮手腕怎麼脫臼的？

A）她出車禍。

B）她遇到飛機失事。

C）她遇到船難。

D）她發生運 傷害。

Chapter

4

ntersection	n.	十字路口
broken	adj.	破的，碎裂的
wrist	n.	手腕

Chapter
1

Chapter
2

Chapter
3

Chapter
4

Chapter
5

Chapter
6

Chapter
7

Chapter
8

Chapter
9

Chapter
10

Unit 2　Keeping Friends
珍惜友誼

Anne is sitting at a table in a restaurant. Ted comes in and joins her.
安妮坐在餐廳的桌前，泰德過來和她坐在一起。

 Anne安妮　 Ted泰德

Anne:　How are you Ted?
　　　　你好嗎，泰德？

Ted:　I'm good. How are you?
　　　　很好，妳呢？

Anne:　I'm good.
　　　　很好。

Ted:　Your wrist has healed.
　　　　妳的手腕好了。

Anne:　Yes, it has. I was very lucky that I only got a broken wrist.
　　　　是啊，幸好只是手腕脫臼。

Ted: I'm glad too. I would've been upset to lose you. We need to keep our friends.
我也很高興，如果妳怎麼了，我一定會很難過。朋友要彼此珍惜。

Anne: Speaking of friends, do you have Bill's email address?
說到朋友，你有比爾的電子郵件地址嗎？

Ted: Yes, I do.
有啊。

Anne: Could you please tell me what it is?
能不能告訴我？

Ted: Of course, just let me find it. I have it in here somewhere.
當然，我找找看，我寫在某個地方。

Ted looks through his book.
泰德翻了翻他的書。

Anne: I'm surprised that you're looking in your book.
真訝異，你居然會翻書。

Ted: I don't have it memorized. Where else

would I keep it?

我沒有把它背起來，我會把它寫在哪裡呢？

Anne: You could save it in your computer.

你可以把它存在電腦裡。

Ted: Really?

真的？

Anne: That way you have all your email addresses where you need them, not in a book.

這樣你可以把所有的郵件地址都放在需要用到的地方，而不是寫在書裡。

Ted: I didn't know that you could do that.

我不知道可以這樣做。

Anne: Yes. There's an address book in your email account.

是的，你的郵件帳號裡有一個通訊錄。

Anne opens her notebook.
安妮打開她的筆記型電腦。

Anne: Do you see that tool bar?

有沒有看到那個工具列？

Chapter 1

Chapter 2

Chapter 3

Chapter 4

Chapter 5

Chapter 6

Chapter 7

Chapter 8

Chapter 9

Chapter 10

Ted: Yes.
有。

Anne: Read the buttons in that tool bar to me.
把工具列裡的按鈕名稱唸給我聽。

Ted: Well, there's "create mail"...
呃，有「新增郵件」…

Anne: Yes.
沒錯。

Ted: And "reply" and "forward"...
還有「回覆」和「轉寄」。

Anne: Go on.
繼續。

Ted: And "addresses"! Anne, you know everything!
還有「通訊錄」！安妮，妳真是個萬事通！

Anne: Of course, I don't. But I do know that it's important to keep good friends.
我當然不是，但我知道珍惜好朋友是很重要的事。

Ted: In my address book.
放到我的通訊錄裡。

Anne: That's right, Ted. Use a computer instead of the book you keep in your book bag.
對啦，泰德。要用電腦，而不是你放在書包裡的書。

Ted: That will be much more convenient.
這樣就方便多了。

Anne: Now, can I please have Bill's email address?
我現在可以知道比爾的電子郵件地址了吧。

Ted: Yes, of course. Do you want me to write it down for you?
當然，要我寫給妳嗎？

Anne: Yes, please. I won't remember it unless you do.
好啊，要不然我記不住。

> Ted writes it down and gives it to Anne.
> 泰德把地址寫下來，交給安妮。

Ted: Here it is.
給妳。

Anne: Thank you.
謝謝。

Chapter 1
Chapter 2
Chapter 3
Chapter 4
Chapter 5
Chapter 6
Chapter 7
Chapter 8
Chapter 9
Chapter 10

Ted: You're welcome. What do you need it for?
不客氣。妳要這個做什麼？

Anne: I'm going to send an email to Bill.
我要寫一封信給他。

Ted: I guessed that. Why do you want to email him?
我想也是。妳為什麼要寫信給他呢？

Anne: It's just like you said before. It's important to keep your friends.
就像你剛剛説的，朋友要好好珍惜。

Ted: It would be nice if all four of us could do something fun together.
如果我們四個人一起出去，一定很好玩。

Anne: Do you mean me and you and Bill and Kara?
你是説我、你、比爾和卡拉？

Ted: Yes. Don't you think it'd be fun for all of us to go to a movie tonight?
嗯。妳覺得今晚我們一起去看電影，怎麼樣？

Chapter
1

Chapter
2

Chapter
3

Chapter
4

Chapter
5

Chapter
6

Chapter
7

Chapter
8

Chapter
9

Chapter
10

Anne: I think that would be lots of fun. I will email Bill and Kara about it.

我想那一定很好玩。我寫電子郵件去問比爾和卡拉。

Ted: And I will see what movies are playing tonight. Bye for now, Anne.

我去查查看今晚有什麼電影。先拜拜了，安妮。

Anne: See you later, Ted.

待會見，泰德。

____1. Where does Ted Keep his email addresses?
A) In a book in his book bag
B) In his head
C) In his pocket
D) In his underwear

____2. How is Anne's wrist?
A) It has turned green.
B) It is sore.
C) It is broken.
D) It has healed.

____3. When do Anne and Ted want to go a movie?
A) Tomorrow
B) Right now
C) Tonight
D) This afternoon

____4. Why has Ted kept his addresses in a book?
A) He prefers it.
B) He didn't know he could keep them in the computer.
C) He is trying to make a point.
D) He is not very smart.

Answers 解答

<u> A </u> 1. **泰德把電子郵件地址寫在哪裡？**

    A）在他書包裡的書

    B）在他的腦中

    C）在他的皮夾裡

    D）在他的內衣裡

<u> D </u> 2. **安妮的手腕如何？**

    A）它變綠了。

    B）它在發炎。

    C）它脫臼了。

    D）它痊癒了。

<u> C </u> 3. **安妮和泰德何時去看電影？**

    A）明天

    B）現在

    C）今晚

    D）今天下午

<u> B </u> 4. **泰德為何把電子郵件地址寫在書上？**

    A）他比較喜歡這樣。

    B）他不知道他可以把它們記在電腦裡。

    C）他想要表達一些事情。

    D）他不是很聰明。

Chapter
4

Vocabulary 字彙通

tool bar	n.	工具列
addresse	n.	通訊錄

Chapter
1

Chapter
2

Chapter
3

Chapter
4

Chapter
5

Chapter
6

Chapter
7

Chapter
8

Chapter
9

Chapter
10

Unit 3   **More Than One**
好事成雙

Ted is sitting at a table in the cafeteria. Kara sits down with him.
泰德坐在自助餐店的桌前，卡拉和他坐在一起。

👨 Ted泰德   👩 Kara卡拉

Ted: Kara, where is Anne?
卡拉，安妮呢？

Kara: Anne couldn't come.
安妮不能來。

Ted: Why not?
為什麼？

Kara: She forgot that she had a doctor's appointment today. She said to tell you sorry.
她忘記她今天已經和醫生有約，叫我跟你說對不起。

Ted: No problem. You and I can still do

something together, right?

沒問題，我們還是可以一起去做點什麼，對不對？

Kara: Yes. I don't have to be anywhere right now.

對，反正我現在也沒有要去哪裡。

Ted: Great. What do you want to do?

太好了，妳想做什麼？

Kara: We could go bowling.

我們可以去打保齡球。

Ted: I like bowling. That would be fun. Still, it'd be fun if there were more than one.

我喜歡打保齡球，一定很好玩。但是如果有更多人會更好玩。

Kara: How do you mean?

什麼意思？

Ted: It'd be more fun if there were more than one person on each bowling team.

打保齡球時，每隊一個人以上，比較好玩。

Kara: I agree. It's too bad that Anne can't come.

我同意，可惜安妮不能來。

Ted: There would still be only one person on the other team.
這樣另外一隊還是只有一個人。

Kara: We would need more than one person on both teams. That would be the most fun.
每隊都要一個人以上，才會好玩。

Ted: We should see if Bill and Anne could go bowling later. All four of us could play.
我們問問看比爾和安妮待會兒能不能去。這樣我們四個人就可以一起玩。

Kara: Good idea. Let's email them and ask.
好主意，我們寄電子郵件去問他們。

Ted: All right. I'll email Bill and you can send a message to Anne.
好，我寄給比爾，妳寄給安妮。

Ted pulls his laptop out of his book bag.
泰德從書包裡拿出筆記型電腦。

Kara: Why don't you just send a message to both of them?
你為什麼不同時寄給他們兩個人？

Chapter 1
Chapter 2
Chapter 3
Chapter 4
Chapter 5
Chapter 6
Chapter 7
Chapter 8
Chapter 9
Chapter 10

Ted: Wouldn't it be faster if each of us emailed one of them?

我們兩個各寄一封不是比較快嗎？

Kara: It would be fastest if one of us emailed both of them at the same time.

我們其中一個人同時寄給他們兩個，會更快。

Ted: How do you do that?

這要怎麼做？

Kara: You can send one email message to more than one person.

一封電子郵件可以一次寄給很多人。

Ted: Really?

真的？

Kara: You can send the same message to many people at the same time. Watch.

你可以同時寄同一 信給很多人。你看。

Kara opens her notebook.

卡拉打開她的筆記型電腦。

Ted: Okay.

好的。

Kara: I type both Anne and Bill's addresses. I can type in as many addresses as I want.
我同時輸入安妮和比爾的地址。我要打多少個地址都可以。

Ted: Type my address in as well. Then I will get that email also. I love email.
也打上我的地址，這樣我也能收到那封信。我喜歡電子郵件。

Kara: There are so many useful things about email.
電子郵件有很多用處。

Ted: Yes, there are and you just showed me one more.
是啊，妳剛剛又教了我一招。

Kara: I showed you more than one useful thing about email, haven't I?
電子郵件好用的地方，我不只教你一招，對吧？

Ted: Yes, you have.
是啊。

Kara: Well, hopefully we'll bowl tonight with more than one person on each team.
好吧，希望今晚我們打保齡球時，每隊不會只有一個人。

Chapter 1

Chapter 2

Chapter 3

Chapter 4

Chapter 5

Chapter 6

Chapter 7

Chapter 8

Chapter 9

Chapter 10

Ted: Yes. Hopefully both of them will be able to come.

是啊,希望他們兩個都能來。

Kara: Do you know if Bill likes to bowl?

你知道比爾喜歡打保齡球嗎?

Ted: I don't know.

不知道。

Kara: I know that Anne likes to bowl.

我知道安妮喜歡。

Ted: I hope that more than one of them likes to bowl.

希望他們兩個人都喜歡保齡球。

___1. Why didn't Anne come to the cafeteria?

A) She had an exam to write.

B) She had a doctor's appointment to go to.

C) Anne doesn't like Kara.

D) Anne doesn't like Ted.

___2. Who does Ted want to go bowling with?

A) Anne, Kara, and Bill

B) Kara and Bill

C) Anne and Bill

D) Bill

___3. What does Anne send to Bill, Kara, and Ted?

A) Her email address

B) Presents

C) Invitations to go to the prom

D) An email

___4. How come Anne couldn't come?

A) She slept in.

B) Her alarm clock didn't go off.

C) She couldn't get a ride.

D) She had a doctor's appointment.

Answers 解答

 B 1. 安妮為什麼沒有一起去餐廳？

A) 她要寫考卷。

B) 她要去看醫生。

C) 安妮不喜歡卡拉。

D) 安妮不喜歡泰德。

 A 2. 泰德想要和誰去打保齡球？

A) 安妮、卡拉和比爾

B) 卡拉和比爾

C) 安妮和比爾

D) 比爾

 D 3. 安妮送什麼給比爾、卡拉和泰德？

A) 她的電子郵件地址

B) 禮物

C) 舞會的邀請函

D) 一封電子郵件

 D 4. 為何安妮不能來？

A) 她在睡覺。

B) 她的鬧鐘壞了。

C) 沒有人載她。

D) 她已經預約要看醫生了。

Chapter

5

Being Polite

要有禮貌

Unit 1

Making Faces
扮鬼臉

Bill and Anne are watching TV.
比爾和安妮在看電視。

 Bill比爾　 Anne安妮

Bill: Did you have fun bowling last week, Anne?
安妮，妳上星期打保齡球，玩得高不高興？

Anne: I did, Bill. Did you?
高興。你呢，比爾？

Bill: Yes. I like bowling.
高興，我喜歡保齡球。

Anne: Me too.
我也是。

Bill: I had never tried bowling before.
我以前從沒玩過保齡球。

Anne: I have bowled many times. What's the matter? You're making a funny face.
我玩過很多次。怎麼了，你幹嘛扮鬼臉？

Bill: I smell something.
我聞到一股味道。

Anne: What?
什麼？

Bill: It's coming from the kitchen.
從廚房傳來的。

Anne: It smells like something is burning.
好像有東西燒焦了。

Bill: My toast is burning. I'll unplug the toaster. Now, you're the one making a face.
我的吐司燒焦了，我去把烤麵包機插頭拔掉，現在換妳在扮鬼臉了。

> Bill goes into the kitchen to deal with the smoking toaster.
> 比爾到廚房處理冒煙的烤麵包機。

Anne: It's very smoky in here.
這裡到處都是煙。

Bill: I put some bread in the toaster. It must have got stuck.
我放了一些麵包在烤麵包機裡，一定是卡住了。

Anne: Do you want me to open a window?
要不要我把窗戶打開？

Bill: Yes, please.
好的，麻煩妳。

Anne: It's interesting that you brought up making faces.
你剛剛突然扮鬼臉，蠻有趣哦。

Bill: Why is that?
為什麼呢？

Anne: Have you noticed that Ted includes a lot of those faces in his emails?
你有沒有注意到，泰德的信裡有一堆那種鬼臉。

Bill: Ted puts so many "emoticons" in his emails that there's no room left for words.

他在信裡放了太多的「表情符號」，都沒有地方寫字了。

Anne: His emails are hard to read because there are more faces than words.

他的電子郵件好難懂，表情符號比字還多。

Bill: He puts in smiling faces, sad faces, angry faces...

他放了笑臉、哭臉、生氣的臉……

Anne: He puts in scared faces, funny faces, bored faces...

還有可怕的、好笑的、無聊的表情……

Bill: He puts way too many faces in his emails. I should tell him to lay off on the faces.

他實在放了太多的表情符號在信裡面。我應該告訴他，不要再放了。

Chapter 1
Chapter 2
Chapter 3
Chapter 4
Chapter 5
Chapter 6
Chapter 7
Chapter 8
Chapter 9
Chapter 10

> **Bill comes back from the kitchen.**
> 比爾從廚房裡走回來。

Anne: Now, you're making a face again.
你又再扮鬼臉了。

Bill: Yes, I am.
沒錯。

Anne: What kind of face are you making?
你剛剛那是什麼表情？

Bill: What does it look like?
看起來像哪一種？

Anne: It looks like a sad face.
看起來像哭臉。

Bill: You are right.
妳說對了。

Anne: Why are you making a sad face?
為什麼要扮哭臉呢？

Bill: I'm hungry and I burned my toast.
我肚子餓，而我又把我的吐司烤焦了。

Anne: You could just toast some more bread.
你可以再烤一些啊。

Bill: No, I can't. I am all out of bread.
不行，我沒麵包了。

Anne: Well, I guess that we will have to go buy more bread.
那，我們就再去買一點吧。

Bill: I'm making a face again.
我又在做鬼臉了。

Anne: It looks like a happy face to me. Let's go buy some bread.
看起來像是個笑臉，我們去買麵包吧。

Bill: Will you have toast with me?
妳要不要一起吃？

Anne: I will have some toast. I like toast.
我會吃一點，我喜歡吐司。

Bill: I like to put chocolate icing on it. Now you're making a face.
我喜歡放巧克力糖霜在上面。現在妳在扮鬼臉了。

Anne: You're not supposed to put chocolate

Chapter 1

Chapter 2

Chapter 3

Chapter 4

Chapter 5

Chapter 6

Chapter 7

Chapter 8

Chapter 9

Chapter 10

icing on toast. Icing goes on cakes.

你不應該在吐司上放巧克力糖霜的,那是放在蛋糕上的。

Bill: I don't care what you think.

我才不在乎妳的想法呢。

Anne: That wasn't very nice. You hurt my feelings.

你那樣講話很不客氣。你讓我很受傷。

Bill: I know I did. I can see it on your face. I am sorry. Now let's go get some bread.

我知道,看妳的表情就知道,對不起。現在我們去買麵包吧。

___1. Why is there smoke in Bill's kitchen?

A) Anne is smoking.

B) Bill is smoking.

C) The toast is burning.

D) There is a fire in the kitchen.

___2. Who likes chocolate icing on toast?

A) Bill

B) Anne

C) The neighbors

D) Ted

___3. What does Bill need to buy?

A) More chocolate icing

B) A new toaster

C) More toast

D) More bread

___4. Why does Bill look sad?

A) He is hungry.

B) He likes to look sad.

C) He is bored.

D) He is happy.

Answers 解答

<u> C </u> 1. 比爾的廚房裡為什麼有煙？

    A）安妮在抽煙。

    B）比爾在抽煙。

    C）吐司燒焦了。

    D）廚房起火了。

<u> A </u> 2. 誰喜歡在吐司上放巧克力糖霜？

    A）比爾

    B）安妮

    C）鄰居

    D）泰德

<u> D </u> 3. 比爾需要買什麼？

    A）更多巧克力糖霜

    B）一台新烤吐司機

    C）更多吐司

    D）更多麵包

<u> A </u> 4. 為什麼比爾看起來不太高興？

    A）他餓了。

    B）他喜歡看起來很難過。

    C）他覺得很無趣。

    D）他很快樂。

Vocabulary 字彙通

icing   n.   糖霜

Chapter
1

Chapter
2

Chapter
3

Chapter
4

Chapter
5

Chapter
6

Chapter
7

Chapter
8

Chapter
9

Chapter
10

Unit 2

Stop Shouting!
不要再吼了

Bill and Kara are having a snack in Bill's kitchen.
比爾和卡拉在比爾的廚房裡吃點心。

 Bill比爾　　Kara卡拉

Bill: Kara, did you hear about the fire in my kitchen?

卡拉，妳有沒有聽說我廚房失火的事？

Kara: Anne told me that you burned some toast. She didn't tell me that there was a fire.

安妮告訴過我你烤焦了吐司，但沒有跟我說失火的事。

Bill: It was huge.

很嚴重呢！

Kara: I hope there was no damage.

希望沒什麼損傷。

Bill: Only my toast was damaged.
只有我的吐司陣亡了。

Kara: Did you have to call the fire department?
你有沒有必要打電話給消防隊？

Bill: No.
沒有。

Kara: Did you yell to the neighbors for help?
你有沒有大聲叫鄰居來幫忙？

Bill: No.
沒有。

Kara: I don't understand. Those are some things that you should do if there's a fire.
我真不懂。如果失火，你應該想想辦法。

Bill: There wasn't really a fire. I was only joking. I just burned my toast.
那也不算是火災啦，我只是在開玩笑。我只是烤焦我的吐司而已。

Kara: Silly.
傻。

Bill: I hope I never do have a fire. If I shouted at the neighbors, they wouldn't come.

我希望永遠不會碰上火災。如果我對鄰居大叫，他們也不會來。

Kara: Why not?

為什麼呢？

Bill: They're not very friendly. They would only yell at me to stop yelling.

他們不是很友善。他們可能只會吼回來，叫我別再叫了。

Kara: Speaking of yelling and shouting, do you ever get emails from Anne?

說到大吼大叫，你有沒有收到安妮的郵件？

Bill: Yes, I do.

有啊。

Kara: Does she type all of her messages in capital letters?

她是不是都用大寫字體寫郵件？

Bill: Yes, she does.

是的，沒錯。

Chapter 1

Chapter 2

Chapter 3

Chapter 4

Chapter 5

Chapter 6

Chapter 7

Chapter 8

Chapter 9

Chapter 10

Kara: Maybe she doesn't know that people think of that as being yelled at.

也許她不知道，別人看見這種字體時，會以為她在對他們咆哮。

Bill: Probably not.

她可能不知道。

Kara: When I read something that's written all in capital letters, I read it as yelling.

當我看到全部都用大寫字體寫的郵件時，我會以為那是在對我咆哮。

Bill: I think everybody reads it like that.

我想每個人都會有這種想法。

Kara: I don't like being yelled at.

我不喜歡人家對我那樣吼叫。

Bill: I don't like it, either.

我也不喜歡。

Kara: Maybe we should talk to her about that.

也許我們應該跟她談談。

Bill: I have a better idea. Why don't we just email her about it?

我有一個更好的主意，我們為什麼不發電子郵件給她呢？

Kara: Why?
為什麼？

Bill: If we tell her in person, she might get mad.
如果我們當面和她說，她可能會生氣。

Kara: If she gets mad, she might yell at us.
她如果生氣了，可能會對我們大吼大叫。

Bill: What will we say in the email message?
我們信裡要說什麼呢？

Kara: I think that you should write "stop shouting".
我想你應該說「別再咆哮了」。

Bill: Okay.
好啊。

Kara: Why don't you type it all in capital letters?
你要不要都用大寫字體來寫？

Bill: Do you think that she will understand what we're trying to tell her?
你覺得這樣做，她會明白我們的意思嗎？

Kara: I don't know.
我不確定。

Chapter 1

Chapter 2

Chapter 3

Chapter 4

Chapter 5

Chapter 6

Chapter 7

Chapter 8

Chapter 9

Chapter 10

Bill: I don't want to do that if there is a
chance that she'll be hurt.
如果這樣會傷害到她，我不要這樣做。

Kara: Let's say that we like getting emails from
her but writing like that is like shouting.
要不然就說，我們很喜歡收到她的信，但那種寫法好
像在大吼大叫。

Bill: Okay.
好的。

> Kara hears something.
> 卡拉聽到了聲音。

Kara: Do you hear that?
你有沒有聽到什麼聲音？

Bill: It sounds like someone's yelling.
好像有人在叫。

Kara: Where's it coming from?
從哪裡傳來的？

Bill: I'm not sure. I'll look out the window
and see.
不太清楚，我去看看窗外。

Kara: What is it? What do you see?

是什麼呢？你看到了什麼。

Bill: You won't believe me. Better look for yourself.

妳一定不會相信，自己來看看吧。

Kara: There's Anne.

是安妮。

Bill: And there's Ted.

還有泰德。

Kara: And what are they doing?

他們在幹嘛？

Bill: Yelling at us to come down and let them in. I forgot that the doorbell isn't working.

叫我們下去讓他們進來，我忘記我的門鈴壞了。

Kara: At least they didn't throw rocks at the window.

至少他們沒有拿石頭砸玻璃。

Bill: I guess that there is a good time for shouting and yelling after all.

看來，有時候大吼大叫是有必要的。

Chapter 1

Chapter 2

Chapter 3

Chapter 4

Chapter 5

Chapter 6

Chapter 7

Chapter 8

Chapter 9

Chapter 10

___1. Why are Ted and Anne yelling to be
let in?
A) They are rude.
B) They don't know about doorbells.
C) The door bell is broken.
D) The toaster is broken.

___2. Who does Bill say is not friendly?
A) Kara
B) The neighbors
C) The fire department
D) Anne

___3. What does Anne need to stop doing?
A) She needs to stop writing her emails all
in capital letters.
B) She needs to stop sending emails.
C) She needs to stop yelling at Bill.
D) All of the above

___4. How does Bill know that Anne and Ted
are there?
A) He hears the fire department.
B) He hears the neighbors.
C) He hears the toast burning.
D) He hears them yelling.

Answers 解答

_C_ 1. 為什麼泰德和安妮大叫著要進來？

A）他們沒有禮貌。

B）他們不知道門鈴在哪裡。

C）門鈴壞了。

D）烤吐司機壞了。

_B_ 2. 比爾說誰不友善？

A）卡拉

B）鄰居

C）消防隊

D）安妮

_A_ 3. 安妮應該停止什麼樣的行為？

A）她應該停止用大寫字體寫她的電子郵件。

B）她應該停止寄電子郵件。

C）她應該停止對比爾大叫。

D）以上皆是。

_D_ 4. 比爾怎麼知道安妮和泰德在那裡？

A）他聽到消防隊的聲音。

B）他聽到鄰居的聲音。

C）他聽到吐司燒焦的聲音。

D）他聽到他們大叫。

Vocabulary 字彙通

capital letter   n.   大寫字母

Keep it Confidential
噓……

Kara and Anne are walking to the store.
卡拉和安妮走進一家店。

👤 Anne安妮　👤 Kara卡拉

Anne: Kara, I haven't seen you in days.
卡拉，我好幾天沒看到妳了。

Kara: Sorry. I've been very busy.
對不起，我最近很忙。

Anne: What have you been doing?
妳在忙什麼呢？

Kara: It's a secret. I can't tell you yet.
那是秘密，還不能告訴妳。

Anne: Please tell me. I can keep a secret.
告訴我嘛，拜託，我會保密的。

Kara: I know that you can keep a secret but I

can't tell you. Be patient with me. Okay?
我知道妳會保密，但我不能告訴妳，忍耐一下，好嗎？

Anne: Okay. So, what have you been up to?
好吧。那妳最近怎麼樣？

Kara: I've been doing this and that.
忙這個和那個。

Anne: What does "this and that" mean?
「這個和那個」是什麼意思？

Kara: I said that I'm not allowed to tell you yet. You have to wait.
我的意思是我還不能告訴妳，妳要等一等。

Anne: But I don't want to wait.
但我不要等。

Kara: It's not just you. I can't tell anyone yet.
不只是妳，我誰都不能說。

Anne: Not even Bill?
連比爾也不可以？

Kara: Especially not Bill.
尤其是比爾。

Chapter
1

Chapter
2

Chapter
3

Chapter
4

Chapter
5

Chapter
6

Chapter
7

Chapter
8

Chapter
9

Chapter
10

Anne: Oh.
哦……

Kara: Oh what?
哦什麼？

Anne: Nothing.
沒事。

Kara: What do you mean by that?
妳那是什麼意思？

Anne: By what?
什麼什麼？

Kara: What did you mean when you said "nothing"?
妳說「沒事」是什麼意思？

Anne: I think I know what this is all about.
我想我知道這是怎麼回事了

Kara stops walking.
卡拉停了下來。

Kara: You do?
妳知道？

Anne: Yes.
對。

Kara: How would you know?
妳怎麼會知道？

Anne: I received an email from somebody.
我收到某人的電子郵件。

Kara: And what did this email say?
信裡怎麼說？

Anne: I'm beginning to think that Ted sent me an email that he shouldn't have.
我開始在想，泰德寄給我一封他不該寄的電子郵件。

Kara: What did this email from Ted say?
泰德在這封信裡怎麼說？

Anne: He forwarded an email to me that you had sent to him.
他轉寄一封妳寄給他的郵件給我。

Kara: Which email of mine did he forward?
他轉寄了我哪一封郵件？

Anne: The one you talk about throwing a surprise party for Bill.
妳說要幫比爾辦驚喜派對的那封郵件。

Chapter
1

Chapter
2

Chapter
3

Chapter
4

Chapter
5

Chapter
6

Chapter
7

Chapter
8

Chapter
9

Chapter
10

Kara: I can't believe that he forwarded my email to you. That's so rude.

我真不敢相信，他居然把我的信轉寄給妳。真是太沒禮貌。

Anne: It is rude. He didn't ask you first?

真的很沒禮貌。他沒有先問妳嗎？

Kara: No.

沒有。

Anne: Uh oh.

喔喔。

Kara: What?

怎麼了？

Anne: I think that Ted's going to get into a lot of trouble over this.

我想泰德會因為這個而惹上大麻煩了。

Kara: I don't think so. He's the one who said I'm not allowed to tell anyone.

我和妳看法不同。是他叫我不要告訴別人的。

Anne: Well, isn't that funny.

哦，那不是很可笑嗎？

Kara: It's not funny at all.

一點都不好笑。

Anne: I guess that he wanted to break the news himself.

我猜他想要自己宣佈這個消息。

Kara: I want to break something too. His nose.

我也想打破一樣東西，他的鼻子。

Anne: Kara, don't do that.

卡拉，別這麼做。

Kara: I can't believe that he forwarded an email of mine and he did it without asking me.

我真不敢相信，他把我的信轉寄出去，居然沒有問過我。

Anne: And he told you to keep it confidential.

而且他還叫妳保守秘密。

Kara: But he didn't. Well, not only are we throwing a party for Bill.

但他自己卻沒有。好吧，我們不只要幫比爾辦一個派對。

Anne: What else are we going to throw?

我們還要做什麼？

Chapter 1
Chapter 2
Chapter 3
Chapter 4
Chapter 5
Chapter 6
Chapter 7
Chapter 8
Chapter 9
Chapter 10

Kara: I think we are going to throw Ted in the lake.

我想我們要把泰德給扔到湖裡去。

Anne: Now, that's a secret that I am glad to know.

現在，這倒是個我很樂於聽到的秘密。

___1. Why has Anne been too busy to see Kara?

A) She has three part time jobs.

B) She owns five cats that need her care.

C) She hasn't been to busy to see Kara.

D) Anne has been planning a surprise party for Bill.

___2. Who is in trouble?

A) Kara

B) Ted

C) Bill

D) Anne

Chapter

5

___3. What is being planned?

A) A surprise party for Bill

B) Going to a movie

C) Making toast

D) Going bowling

___4. How did Anne find out the secret?

A) Kara told her.

B) Bill forwarded an email to her.

C) Ted told her.

D) Ted forwarded an email to her.

Answers 解答

<u>D</u> 1. **為什麼安妮很忙，沒時間和卡拉碰面？**

A）她有三份兼職工作。

B）她有五隻貓需要她照顧。

C）她沒有忙到不能和卡拉碰面。

D）安妮正在為比爾計畫一個驚喜派對。

<u>B</u> 2. **誰惹禍上身了？**

A）卡拉

B）泰德

C）比爾

D）安妮

<u>A</u> 3. **什麼計畫在進行著？**

A）為比爾舉辦的驚喜派對

B）看電影

C）做吐司

D）打保齡球

<u>D</u> 4. **安妮是怎麼發現秘密的？**

A）卡拉告訴她的。

B）比爾轉寄一封電子郵件給她。

C）泰德告訴她的。

D）泰德轉寄一封電子郵件給她。

| confidential | adj. | 機密的，秘密的 |
| rude | adj. | 魯的，不禮貌的 |

Chapter
5

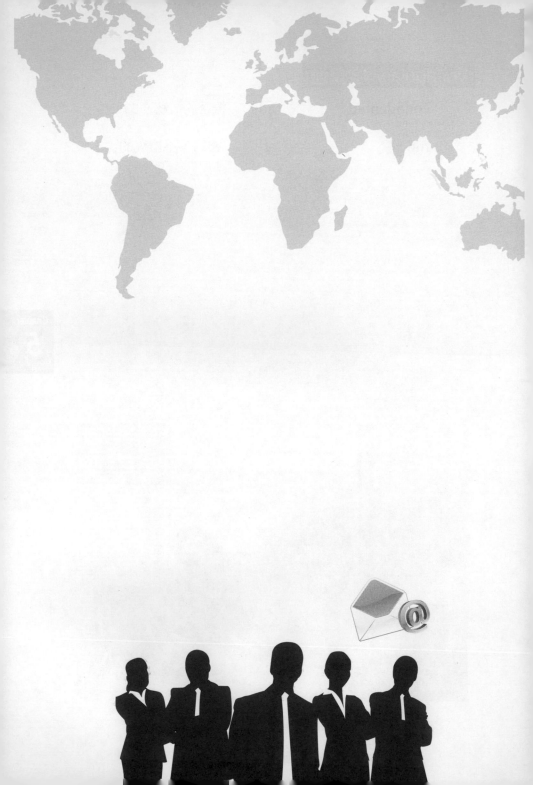

Chapter

6

Something is Missing
人不見了

To Email or Not to Email
要寄？還是不寄？

> Bill sees Kara in the grocery store and goes over to her.
> 比爾在雜貨店看到卡拉，於是就走了過去。

　　👤 Bill比爾　　👤 Kara卡拉

Bill: Kara, have you seen Ted?
卡拉，妳有沒有看到泰德？

Kara: I haven't seen Ted in a long time, Bill. When's the last time you saw him?
我好久沒看到泰德了，比爾。你上次看到他是什麼時候？

Bill: I can't remember. It's been quite a while.
我不記得了，蠻久了。

Kara: I wonder what's going on. I wonder where he is.
不知道發生了什麼事，不曉得他人在哪裡。

Bill: Anne hasn't seen Ted either.
安妮也沒有看到泰德。

Kara: How long has it been since she saw him?
她多久沒看到他了？

Bill: She didn't say.
她沒說。

Kara: I hope that he's all right.
希望他沒事。

Bill: I'm sure that he's fine.
我想他一定沒事。

Kara: How do you know?
你怎麼會知道？

Bill: He emails me all the time.
他一直有寄電子郵件給我。

Kara: Well, he's emailing me too. But that doesn't mean that everything's fine.
沒錯，他也寄給我了。但這不表示他沒事。

Bill: What do you mean?
這話什麼意思？

Chapter 1

Chapter 2

Chapter 3

Chapter 4

Chapter 5

Chapter 6

Chapter 7

Chapter 8

Chapter 9

Chapter 10

Kara: If everything were fine, he would come see us.

如果沒事，他會來看我們。

Bill: I suppose.

應該是這樣。

Kara: If everything were okay, he would phone.

如果沒事，他會打電話來。

Bill: I wonder if he's become addicted to email.

我在想他是不是對電子郵件上癮了。

Kara: How can anyone be addicted to email? It's not a drug.

怎麼可能有人對電子郵件上癮？那又不是毒品。

Bill: People get addicted to anything. They start thinking they don't need to see people.

人有可能對任何東西上癮。他們開始覺得自己不需要再跟人們碰面。

Kara: I was like that for a while. I didn't want to talk to anyone on the phone.

我有一陣子也是那樣。我不想和任何人通電話。

Bill: Yes.
對。

Kara: I didn't want to go see people. It seemed like too much work.
我不想和任何人碰面，覺得那樣太麻煩。

Bill: Uh huh.
沒錯。

Kara: Email was great. I didn't have to get dressed or bathe before I talked to someone.
電子郵件真的很棒。和別人交談前，我不必先穿戴整齊或梳洗乾淨。

Bill: I think that's what Ted's going through. He'd rather email someone than see them.
我猜泰德正經歷那個階段。他寧可傳信件，也不想見到人們。

Kara: That is what you mean when you say "addicted to email"?
這就是你所謂「對電子郵件上癮」？

Bill: Yes.
是的。

Chapter 1
Chapter 2
Chapter 3
Chapter 4
Chapter 5
Chapter 6
Chapter 7
Chapter 8
Chapter 9
Chapter 10

Kara: I'm worried about Ted. What do we do?

我很擔心泰德，我們該怎麼辦？

Bill: Nothing. He'll grow out of it, hopefully. He'll get lonely.

什麼事也不用做，他會戒掉的，希望如此。他會覺得寂寞。

Kara: Like you said, hopefully.

就像你說的，希望如此。

Bill: He will. And when he gets lonely, he'll start to phone and email us again.

他會的。等他覺得寂寞，就會開始打電話或發信件給我們。

Kara: How do you know?

你怎麼知道？

Bill: I know because I went through it myself. You went through it too.

我知道，因為我也曾經歷過那個階段。妳也是啊。

Kara: Yes.

沒錯。

Bill: I think that most people go through this when they learn how to use email.

我想大部分剛學會電子郵件的人，都經歷過這個階段。

Kara: All this talk about choosing email over people has made me feel lonely.

談到選擇郵件比人重要這件事，突然讓我覺得有點寂寞。

Bill: Let's email Anne and see if she'll meet us for supper.

我們寫信給安妮，看她要不要和我們一起吃晚餐。

Kara: Let's phone Anne and see if she'll meet us for supper.

我們打電話給安妮，看她要不要和我們一起吃晚餐。

Bill: Phone her?

打電話給她？

Kara: Yes. Let's phone her instead of sending an email.

是啊，我們打電話給她，不要發郵件了。

Bill: Good idea, Kara. Here's my phone. Why don't you call her?

好主意，卡拉。這是我的電話。妳何不打給她？

Kara: Thanks, Bill. You're a good friend.

謝謝，比爾，你真是一個好朋友。

Chapter 1

Chapter 2

Chapter 3

Chapter 4

Chapter 5

Chapter 6

Chapter 7

Chapter 8

Chapter 9

Chapter 10

Bill: You're a good friend too. Will you buy me supper?

妳也是一個好朋友。要不要請我吃晚餐啊？

Kara: No.

才不要呢。

Bill: Darn it.

真是的。

___1. Where are Bill and Kara?
A) At Bill's house
B) At Kara's house
C) At school
D) At the grocery stores

___2. How does Kara feel?
A) Happy
B) Lonely
C) Angry
D) Special

___3. Why does Bill give Kara his phone?

Chapter
6

A) So that she can call him.
B) So that she can call Ted.
C) So that she can call Anne.
D) So that she can call Anne and Ted.

Answers 解答

_D_ 1. 比爾和卡拉在哪裡？

A）在比爾家

B）在卡拉家

C）在學校

D）在雜貨店

_B_ 2. 卡拉感覺如何？

A）開心的

B）寂寞的

C）生氣的

D）特別的

_C_ 3. 比爾為何把他的電話拿給卡拉？

A）這樣她就可以打電話給他。

B）這樣她就可以打電話給泰德。

C）這樣她就可以打電話給安妮。

D）這樣她就可以打電話給安妮和泰德。

Vocabulary 字彙通

| grocery store | n. | 雜貨店 |
| addicted | adj. | （對…）上癮的 |

Chapter
1

Chapter
2

Chapter
3

Chapter
4

Chapter
5

Chapter
6

Chapter
7

Chapter
8

Chapter
9

Chapter
10

Unit 2

Missing in Action
忙到不見人影

Kara and Anne are looking at clothes in the store.
卡拉和安妮在店裡看衣服。

♀ Anne安妮   ♀ Kara卡拉

Anne: Kara, what do you think that Ted does all day?
卡拉，妳覺得泰德整天在做什麼？

Kara: I think Ted is surfing the Internet a lot. I think he's chatting online with people.
我想他常常上網，在線上和人聊天。

Anne: Yes?
是嗎？

Kara: He's probably playing a lot of games and looking for things to forward to people.
他可能打一堆電動遊戲，找東西轉寄給別人。

Anne: When you're looking for things to forward, what do you look for?

妳在找東西轉寄給他人時，都找什麼樣的東西？

Kara: Jokes, funny pictures, funny news stories, tests and quizzes to do for fun.

笑話、有趣的照片、有趣的新故事、好玩的測驗或猜謎。

Anne: Where do you find these things?

妳到哪裡找這些東西？

Kara: On the Internet.

網路上。

Anne: Do you think Ted is addicted to the Internet also?

妳覺得泰德也對網際網路上癮了嗎？

Kara: I think Ted has found a whole new world that he didn't know about before.

我覺得泰德有發現新大陸的感覺。

Anne: Yes?

真的嗎？

Kara: He's exploring it. He just doesn't realize how much time he spends exploring it.

他在探索這一切。他只是不知道自己花了多少時間探索它而已。

Anne: Do you think we should be worried?
妳覺得我們需要擔心他嗎？

Kara: No. It's like what Bill said. He went through this.
不需要。就像比爾說的，他會度過這一切。

Anne: He did?
他真的這麼說嗎？

Kara: He reminded me that I went through it. You probably did too.
他讓我想起自己以前也是這樣，妳可能也是。

Anne: Hmm.
嗯。

Kara: You went through this when you first learned how to use email, right?
妳剛學會電子郵件時也有這樣的經驗，對不對？

Anne: Yes, I guess I did.
應該是吧。

Kara: That is why we don't need to worry. It's normal.
所以沒有什麼好擔心的，這很正常。

Chapter
1

Chapter
2

Chapter
3

Chapter
4

Chapter
5

Chapter
6

Chapter
7

Chapter
8

Chapter
9

Chapter
10

Anne: I don't know if I agree with that.
我不知道自己同不同意妳的看法。

Kara: It's not normal to spend so much time on the computer and so little with people.
花這麼多時間在電腦上，而不在人身上，這是不正常的。

Anne: Go on.
繼續説。

Kara: Ted will get over this phase he' going through.
泰德會走出這個必經的階段。

Anne: Then the computer will just be a useful tool to him.
然後電腦對他而言，只會變成一種有用的工具。

Kara: Right.
對。

Anne: It will no longer take up all his time.
電腦就不會再佔用他所有的時間。

Kara: Exactly.
正是如此。

Anne: I'm looking forward to that.

我很期待那一天。

Kara: Me too. I miss my friend.
我也是，我很想念我的朋友。

Anne: Our friend who is missing.
我們失蹤的朋友。

Kara: Yes. I miss our friend who's missing.
沒錯，我很想念我們失蹤的朋友。

Anne: Check your email. I'm sure that you will find a message from him.
檢查一下妳的郵件，我想妳一定會收到他的信。

Kara opens her notebook.
卡拉打開她的筆記型電腦。

Kara: You were right. Here's a message from Ted.
妳說對了，有一封泰德的信。

Anne: What does it say?
信上說什麼？

Kara: It says, "Hi, Kara. It seems like I haven't seen you for a long time."
信上說：「嗨，卡拉，好像很久沒見到妳了」。

Chapter 1

Chapter 2

Chapter 3

Chapter 4

Chapter 5

Chapter 6

Chapter 7

Chapter 8

Chapter 9

Chapter 10

Anne: That's a good sign.

那是個好現象。

Kara: It says, "I miss you. I miss Anne too. We should all hang out and do something."

它說：「我想念妳，也想念安妮，我們應該一起出去，做些什麼事」。

Anne: You were right. This must just be a phase that he's going through.

妳說對了，這只是他必經的階段。

Kara: It's just like Bill said. Ted will get lonely and then he will start to phone again.

就像比爾說的，泰德會覺得寂寞，然後他會開始打電話。

Anne: From the way that this email sounds, he's already starting to get lonely.

從這封郵件內容看起來，他已經開始覺得寂寞了。

Kara: That's good. Let's make him miss us even more.

很好，我們要讓他更想我們。

Anne: How do we do that?

要怎麼做呢？

Kara: Let's email him back about all of the fun things that we have been doing.

我們回信告訴他，我們做了哪些好玩的事。

Anne: What fun things?

什麼好玩的事？

Kara: Very funny.

非常好玩的事。

Chapter 1

Chapter 2

Chapter 3

Chapter 4

Chapter 5

Chapter 6

Chapter 7

Chapter 8

Chapter 9

Chapter 10

____1. Who is Kara talking to?

A) Ted

B) Anne

C) Bill

D) Herself

____2. Who is Kara talking about?

A) Ted and Bill

B) Anne

C) Bill

D) Herself

____3. Who is Anne worried about?

A) Ted

B) Kara

C) Bill

D) Herself

____4. What is Ted doing all day?

A) He is exploring the computer.

B) He is exploring Canada.

C) He is exploring his bedroom.

D) He is sleeping.

Answers 解答

__B__ 1. **卡拉在和誰說話？**

A）泰德

B）安妮

C）比爾

D）她自己

__A__ 2. **卡拉在談論誰？**

A）泰德和比爾

B）安妮

C）比爾

D）她自己

__A__ 3. **安妮擔心誰？**

A）泰德

B）卡拉

C）比爾

D）她自己

__A__ 4. **泰德整天在做什麼？**

A）他在探索電腦。

B）他在探索加拿大。

C）他在探索他的房間。

D）他在睡覺。

Vocabulary 字彙通

surf   v.   在電腦網路上瀏覽

Unit 3

The Three Musketeers
三個臭皮匠

> Bill and Anne are walking to the movie store.
>
> 比爾和安妮正往電影院走去。

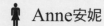 Bill比爾　　 Anne安妮

Bill: I don't like it when Ted doesn't come out with us.

泰德不和我們一起出來，感覺真不好。

Anne: Neither do I. I miss him.

我也是，我很想念他。

Bill: When it's only the three of us, it feels like someone's missing.

只有我們三個，好像少了一個人似的。

Anne: That's what I think also. We're like the Three Musketeers without Ted.

我也這麼想，我們好像是「少了泰德」的三個臭皮匠。

Bill: He may be annoying but he's a lot of fun.

他雖然很煩人，但是很有趣。

Anne: Yes. I've barely heard his voice on the phone at all lately.

是啊，我最近幾乎都沒接到他的電話。

Bill: He just stays in his house and plays on his computer all day.

他整天只待在家裡玩電腦。

Anne: I never see him any more. He emails people from all over the world.

我都沒看到他了，他發電子郵件給世界各地的人。

Bill: How does he know all of these people?

他怎麼會認識這些人？

Anne: He met them online. He emails them and plays computer games.

他在線上遇到他們。他發電子郵件給他們，跟他們打電動。

Bill: He's always been very friendly. I wish he'd come play some real games with us.

他一直都很友善，我希望他來和我們玩一些真實的遊戲。

Chapter 1

Chapter 2

Chapter 3

Chapter 4

Chapter 5

Chapter 6

Chapter 7

Chapter 8

Chapter 9

Chapter 10

Anne: Exactly.
沒錯。

Bill: We haven't gone bowling in a long time. He hasn't come to a movie in a long time.
我們好久沒去打保齡球了。他也好久沒來看電影了。

Anne: I don't think that he annoys them like he annoys us.
我不認為他會去煩那些人，像他煩我們那樣。

Bill: Who?
哪些人？

Anne: The people that he has met by computer.
那些他在電腦上遇到的人。

Bill: You're right. It's hard to annoy people online. It's easy to annoy them in person.
妳說的對。要在線上煩人很難，面對面就很容易了。

Anne: They don't know the real Ted. Besides, those people aren't real friends.
他們不認識真實的泰德。再說，那些人也不是真實的朋友。

Bill: They're only email buddies.

他們只是電子郵件夥伴。

Anne: We're his real friends. Maybe we should go online and play games with him.

我們才是他真正的朋友，也許我們該上線和他玩電動。

Bill: No. Ted needs real friends in the real world.

不行，泰德需要真實世界裡的真實朋友。

Anne: Right. He needs us to be here when he decides to unplug from his computer.

對，當他決定拔掉電腦開關時，需要我們在他身邊。

Bill: Besides, all that computer stuff is boring.

再說，那些電腦玩意還真是無聊。

Anne: Yes. I'd rather see my friends than see words they type to me.

是啊，我寧願親眼見到我的朋友，也不願看到他們打的字。

Anne: You can't live on a computer. Computers and email are only tools.

你不能活在電腦裡。電腦和郵件只是工具。

Chapter 1

Chapter 2

Chapter 3

Chapter 4

Chapter 5

Chapter 6

Chapter 7

Chapter 8

Chapter 9

Chapter 10

Bill: He thinks all you need is a computer and then you will have friends.
他以為只要有電腦，就會有朋友。

Anne: Email is still new to him and he hasn't become used to it yet.
電子郵件對他來說還很新鮮，他還沒習慣。

Bill: And because we're such good friends, we'll be patient.
既然我們都是他的好朋友，我們要耐心等待。

Anne: Yes. And wait for him to get over his email and Internet fascination.
沒錯，我們會等他對電子郵件和網路的新鮮感過去。

Bill: Yes. And while we wait, we'll be the Three Musketeers.
對，在等他的同時，我們只好先做三個臭皮匠啦。

Anne: Let's go find Kara.
我們去找卡拉吧。

Bill: Okay. All for one...
好吧，人人為我…

Anne: And one for all.
我為人人。

___1. Who are Bill and Anne talking about?

    A) They are talking about themselves.

    B) They are talking about Kara.

    C) They are talking about the Three Musketeers.

    D) They are talking about Ted.

___2. What has happened to Bill, Kara, and Anne?

    A) They have not seen a movie all day.

    B) Nothing has happened to them.

    C) They have not had much contact with Ted.

    D) They went bowling.

Chapter 6

___3. Where are Ted and Kara?

    A) They are in the army.

    B) We do not know for sure.

    C) It is not made clear.

    D) Both B and C are correct.

___4. How is Anne feeling?

    A) She is worried about Ted.

    B) She is worried about Bill.

C) She is angry at Kara.

D) She is angry at herself.

Answers 解答

__D__ 1. 比爾和安妮在談論誰？

A）他們在談論他們自己。

B）他們在談論卡拉。

C）他們在談論三個臭皮匠。

D）他們在談論泰德。

__C__ 2. 比爾、卡拉和安妮怎麼了？

A）他們一整天都沒看電影。

B）他們沒有發生任何事。

C）他們很久沒有聯絡到泰德。

D）他們去打保齡球。

__D__ 3. 泰德和卡拉在哪裡？

A）他們在軍隊裡。

B）我們不確定。

C）沒有說清楚。

D）B和C皆正確。

__A__ 4. 安妮感覺如何？

A）她擔心泰德。

B）她擔心比爾。

C）她在氣卡拉。

D）她在氣她自己。

Vocabulary 字彙通

| musketeer | n. | 步兵 |
| fascination | n. | 迷戀 |

Chapter
6

Chapter

7

Threre's a Problem
有問題了

Tell it Like it is
照實說吧

Ted sees Kara at the bus stop and walks up to her.
泰德看到卡拉在公車站，就向她走去。

🧍 Ted泰德　　🧍 Kara卡拉

Ted: Hello, Kara.
哈囉，卡拉。

Kara: Oh! Hello, Ted. It's so nice to see you. I haven't seen you in so long.
哦！哈囉，泰德。真高興看到你，好久不見。

Ted: It's good to see you too.
我也很高興看到妳。

Kara: What're you doing here?
你在這裡做什麼？

Ted: It's been so long since I last saw you.
好久沒看到妳了。

Kara: It has.
是啊。

Ted: I was thinking of you and thought I should come see you.
我很想念妳，覺得應該來看看妳。

Kara: I'm glad that you did. What have you been up to?
我很高興你過來。最近在忙些什麼呢？

Ted: Not much.
沒什麼。

Kara: Isn't there anything new and exciting that you can tell me?
有沒有什麼新鮮、好玩的事要告訴我？

Ted: I can't seem to think of anything.
想不出來有什麼事。

Kara: Have you been bowling?
你有去打保齡球嗎？

Ted: No, I haven't.
沒有。

Kara: Have you seen any good movies lately?
最近有沒有看什麼好電影呢？

Chapter 1
Chapter 2
Chapter 3
Chapter 4
Chapter 5
Chapter 6
Chapter 7
Chapter 8
Chapter 9
Chapter 10

Ted: I can't remember any.

記不起來了。

Kara: Well Ted. What have you been doing with yourself?

那泰德，你最近都在做些什麼呢？

Ted: I don't know. I've been working a lot.

我不知道，做了一大堆事。

Kara: What have you been doing in your spare time?

那你有空時，都在做什麼呢？

Ted: I go online. I email friends and chat online with friends and play games.

我上網、寄信給朋友、和朋友在網上聊天、打電玩。

Kara: Oh. That's nice.

哦，不錯嘛。

Ted: It's all right, I guess. I surf a lot too.

我想還好吧，我也常上網際網路。

Kara: You surf the Internet?

你瀏覽網際網路？

Ted: Yes.

對。

Kara: What do you look for?

你在找什麼嗎？

Ted: There are lots of things to look at. I found the words to some of my favorite songs.

有很多可以看的。我還找到一些我很喜歡的歌曲的歌詞。

Kara: Good for you.

這很好啊。

Ted: So what about you, Kara? What have you been up to?

妳呢，卡拉？妳最近在忙些什麼？

Kara: Lots. I've tried some new restaurants, seen new movies, and went camping.

一堆事。去一些新餐廳、看一些新電影，還去露營。

Kara checks her watch.

卡拉看了看手錶。

Ted: Camping?

露營？

Kara: Yes.

是啊。

Chapter 1

Chapter 2

Chapter 3

Chapter 4

Chapter 5

Chapter 6

Chapter 7

Chapter 8

Chapter 9

Chapter 10

Ted: Does that ever sound like fun.
聽起來好像蠻好玩的。

Kara: It was. I saw a bear and a rabbit.
是很好玩啊，我看到一隻熊和一隻兔子。

Ted: Neat.
酷。

Kara: We went fishing also. I've gone to the museum and to some art galleries also.
我們還去釣魚。我也去了博物館和一些畫廊。

Ted: You've been doing a lot of things. They all sound interesting.
妳做了好多事，聽起來都很有趣。

Kara: It's been a fun summer. We even went horseback riding.
這個夏天玩得很愉快，我們還去騎馬呢。

Ted: I've never been on a horse. Was it fun?
我沒騎過馬，好玩嗎？

Kara: It was terrific. We had such a good time.
棒極了，大家都玩得好愉快。

Ted: I really haven't gotten out much this summer.

我這個夏天幾乎都沒有出門。

Kara: I know. I've missed you. All three of us have missed you.
我知道。我很想念你。我們三個都很想念你。

Ted: Come on. We see each other all the time.
得了吧，我們常常見面的。

Kara: No. I see Anne and Bill all the time. I can't remember when I last saw you.
沒有啊，我常常看到安妮和比爾，我都不記得上次見到你是什麼時候。

Ted: Come on. It hasn't been that long.
得了吧，沒那麼久。

Kara: When was the last time we saw each other Ted?
我們上次見面是什麼時候，泰德？

Ted: I can't remember.
我不記得了。

Kara: That's my point.
這就是啦。

Ted: I should probably get going.
我該走了。

Chapter 1

Chapter 2

Chapter 3

Chapter 4

Chapter 5

Chapter 6

Chapter 7

Chapter 8

Chapter 9

Chapter 10

Kara: Whatever, Ted.

隨便吧，泰德。

Ted: Kara, are you mad at me?

卡拉，妳生我氣了嗎？

Kara: I'm disappointed.

我很失望。

Ted: Tell me what's wrong.

告訴我哪裡不對勁。

Kara: You wasting your life on the computer is what's wrong.

你把生命浪費在電腦上，這就不對。

Ted: I see.

我懂了。

Kara: There's more to life than email, Ted. I have to go now.

人生不只是電子郵件，泰德。我要走了。

Ted: All right I guess.

好吧。

Kara: I have a life to live and people to see and places to go and new things to try.

我還有生活要過、人要見、地方要去，和新鮮事要做。

Ted: Fine. Be mad.

好，那妳就生氣吧。

Kara: Fine. I will.

好，我會的。

___1. Who has tried some new restaurants?
   A) Ted
   B) Anne
   C) Kara
   D) Bill

___2. What did Kara see when she went camping?
   A) A rabbit
   B) A bear
   C) A moose
   D) Both A and B

___3. Where did Ted go this summer?
   A) Camping
   B) Nowhere
   C) Fishing
   D) Horse back riding

___4. How does Kara feel?
   A) She is disappointed.
   B) She is hungry.
   C) She is sad.
   D) She is happy.

Answers 解答

 C 1. 誰去嘗試了新的餐廳？

   A）泰德

   B）安妮

   C）卡拉

   D）比爾

 D 2. 卡拉去露營時看到什麼？

   A）一隻兔子

   B）一隻熊

   C）一隻麋鹿

   D）A和B皆是

 B 3. 泰德這個夏天去哪裡？

   A）露營

   B）沒有去哪裡

   C）釣魚

   D）騎馬

Chapter

7

 A 4. 卡拉感覺如何

   A）她覺得失望。

   B）她覺得生氣。

   C）她覺得難過。

   D）她覺得開心。

gallery	n.	畫廊，美術館
horseback riding		騎馬
terrific	adj.	極好的

Chapter
1

Chapter
2

Chapter
3

Chapter
4

Chapter
5

Chapter
6

Chapter
7

Chapter
8

Chapter
9

Chapter
10

Unit 2

How Interesting
好有趣呢

Anne is sitting on a bench. Ted comes and sits beside her.
安妮坐在長椅子上，泰德過來，坐在她旁邊。

🚹 Ted泰德　　🚺 Anne安妮

Ted: Anne!
安妮！

Anne: Hi, Ted. It's been a long time since I've seen you.
嗨，泰德，好久不見了。

Ted: It hasn't been that long, has it?
沒那麼久吧，有嗎？

Anne: Oh, I think that it's been quite a while.
我覺得很久了。

Ted: Well, never mind that. Tell me what you've been up to this summer.
好吧，算我沒說。談談妳這個夏天在忙些什麼吧。

Anne: I've done lots. I've gone to lots of interesting places.

我做了好多事，去了好多有趣的地方。

Ted: Yes?

真的？

Anne: I've met many interesting people.

遇到很多有趣的人。

Ted: How interesting.

真有意思。

Anne: What have you done all summer, Ted?

你整個夏天都在做什麼呢，泰德？

Ted: I've also done many interesting things and met many interesting people.

我也做了很多有趣的事，認識了很多有趣的人。

Anne: How interesting. What did you do? Who did you meet?

真有意思。你做了什麼？認識了誰？

Ted: I played a lot of games. I met a lot of people playing those games.

我玩了很多電玩，碰到很多也玩那些電動的人。

Anne: Are you talking about computer games?
你是説電腦遊戲？

Ted: Yes.
對。

Anne: And these people you met, did you meet them online?
那些你認識的人，都是在網路上碰到的？

Ted: Yes. So what?
是啊，那又怎樣？

Anne: Do you know what any of them look like?
你知道他們長什麼樣子嗎？

Ted: You think you're so smart, don't you?
妳覺得妳自己很聰明，是不是？

Anne: I think you spend too much time online and not enough time in the real world.
我覺得你花了太多時間上網，太少時間活在真實世界裡。

Ted: Is that so?
是這樣嗎？

Chapter 1

Chapter 2

Chapter 3

Chapter 4

Chapter 5

Chapter 6

Chapter 7

Chapter 8

Chapter 9

Chapter 10

Anne: I think that you aren't spending nearly enough time with your friends.

我覺得你和朋友在一起的時間不夠。

Ted: I spend plenty of time with them.

我花了很多時間和他們在一起。

Anne: I'm talking about us, your real friends, not your computer friends.

我是說我們，你真實的朋友，不是你電腦裡的朋友。

Ted: Wait a minute. The friends that I've made online are real friends.

等一下，我在網路上交的都是真實的朋友。

Anne: Then how come I haven't met them?

那我怎麼都沒碰到他們？

Ted starts to look uncomfortable.
泰德開始看起來有些不自在。

Ted: I don't know.

我不知道。

Anne: How come you haven't introduced them to Bill? To Kara?

你怎麼都沒有把他們介紹給比爾？給卡拉？

Ted: I don't know what to say.
我不知道該說什麼。

Anne: That's because you know I'm right.
You've done nothing all summer.
因為你知道我是對的。你一個夏天什麼都沒做。

Ted: No.
不是這樣的。

Anne: You just sat inside through all this
beautiful weather and played on the
computer.
你只坐在屋裡玩電腦，白白浪費了這麼好的天氣。

Ted: So?
那又怎樣？

Anne: That's sad. That's not how we're supposed
to be living our lives.
那很悲哀。那不是我們該過的生活。

Ted: Who says?
誰說的？

Anne: How interesting can it be sitting in the
same room, in the same house?
坐在同一個屋子裡的同一間房間裡，有什麼好玩的？

Chapter 1

Chapter 2

Chapter 3

Chapter 4

Chapter 5

Chapter 6

Chapter 7

Chapter 8

Chapter 9

Chapter 10

Ted: Whatever.
隨妳怎麼說。

Anne: Looking at the same computer screen, playing the same games?
看著同樣的電腦螢幕，玩同樣的遊戲？

Ted: I play different games.
我有玩不同的遊戲。

Anne: You need to come outside. Smell the fresh air. See your friends. Go bowling.
你需要到戶外走走。去呼吸新鮮空氣、看看朋友、打打保齡球。

Ted: I do.
我有啊。

Anne: When's the last time you actually talked to someone instead of typing to them?
你上次和人面對面說話，我不是說打字，是什麼時候的事了？

Ted: This speech of yours is very interesting but I should be going now.
妳這篇演說很有趣，但我該走了。

Anne: You think about what I said. You need to

Chapter
1

Chapter
2

Chapter
3

Chapter
4

Chapter
5

Chapter
6

Chapter
7

Chapter
8

Chapter
9

Chapter
10

start living and stop being online.
你想想我説的話。你必須開始過生活，別再上網了。

Ted: Yes, yes, yes. I'll think about what you said. Just stop lecturing me, okay?
好、好、好。我會好好想想妳説的話。不要再訓話了，好不好？

Anne: I'll stop lecturing you as soon as you get your life back in order.
只要你回到正常生活，我就不訓你。

Ted: I have to go now.
我現在真的該走了。

Questions 習題

_____ 1. Why is Anne lecturing Ted?

A) She wants him to get some new dance moves.

B) She wants him to learn how to email.

C) She wants him to learn how to sky dive.

D) She wants him to get his life back in order.

_____ 2. Who does Anne say are Ted's real friends?

A) Anne, Kara, and Ted

B) Anne and Ted's computer friends

C) Anne, Ted, and Ted's computer friends

D) Ted doesn't have any real friends.

_____ 3. What did Ted do all summer?

A) He sat in his underwear.

B) He sat in his house and played on the computer.

C) He spent time with Anne.

D) He spent time in the bath tub.

_____ 4. Where does Anne think that Ted needs to go?

A) He needs to come outside.

B) He needs to come to school.

C) He needs to come to work.

D) He needs to come eat pizza.

Answers 解答

__D__ 1. **安妮為何教訓泰德？**

A）她要他學多一點舞蹈動作。

B）她要他學如何寄電子郵件。

C）她要他學會如何跳傘。

D）她要他回到正常生活。

__A__ 2. **安妮說誰是泰德真正的朋友？**

A）安妮、卡拉和泰德

B）安妮和泰德的電腦朋友

C）安妮、泰德，和泰德的電腦朋友

D）泰德不喜歡真實的朋友。

__B__ 3. **泰德整個夏天在做什麼？**

A）他坐在他的內衣裡。

B）他坐在他的房裡玩電腦。

C）他花時間跟安妮在一起。

D）他花時間在浴盆裡。

Chapter
7

A 4. **安妮覺得泰德該去哪裡？**

   A）他應該到外面。

   B）他應該到學校。

   C）他應該去工作。

   D）他應該去吃披薩。

Vocabulary 字彙通

lecture   v.   教訓

Chapter 1
Chapter 2
Chapter 3
Chapter 4
Chapter 5
Chapter 6
Chapter 7
Chapter 8
Chapter 9
Chapter 10

Unit 3   Two is Company
一路有你

Ted is in the computer store. Bill sees him and walks up behind him.
泰德在電腦店裡，比爾看到他，就跟在他後面。

👤 Bill比爾   👤 Ted泰德

Bill: Ted!
泰德！

Ted: Oh, dear. Hi, Bill.
天啊。嗨，比爾。

Bill: What did you say?
你剛剛說了什麼？

Ted: I said, "hi, Bill".
我說：「嗨，比爾」。

Bill: No. Before that.
不，前面那句。

Ted: Nothing. I didn't say anything.

沒有啊，我什麼都沒説。

Bill: Yes you did. You said, "oh dear" like you thought you were in trouble.

有，你説「天啊」，聽起來你好像碰上了麻煩似的。

Ted: Are you going to lecture me like Kara and Anne did?

你也要像卡拉和安妮那樣訓我了嗎？

Bill: No. But I wish you'd come for a walk with me, though. Do you have time?

不。但我希望你和我一起散散步，有空嗎？

Ted: Sure. I'd love to go for a walk with you. It's beautiful outside.

當然，我喜歡和你一起散散步，外面天氣那麼好。

Bill: Yes. The weather has been wonderful. Where should we go?

是啊，最近天氣都很棒。我們要去哪裡呢？

Ted: Let's just see where we end up.

我們看看最後能走到哪兒。

Bill: Okay.

好啊。

Chapter
1

Chapter
2

Chapter
3

Chapter
4

Chapter
5

Chapter
6

Chapter
7

Chapter
8

Chapter
9

Chapter
10

> They leave the store and go outside.
> 他們離開店裡，來到外面。

Bill: What's new with you, Ted?
最近有什麼事嗎，泰德？

Ted: Nothing really. I haven't seen you for a while.
沒什麼。我好久沒看到你了。

Bill: It's good to see you. It's been a long time. What have you been doing?
真高興看到你，好久不見了。最近在忙些什麼呢？

Ted: Not much. I go to work and then I go on the computer when I get home.
沒什麼。我去上班，回到家就打電腦。

Bill: What do you on the computer?
你在電腦上做些什麼呢？

Ted: I email people. I play games and chat with people. I surf.
傳電子郵件給人家、打電玩、和人聊天，到網際網路晃晃。

Bill: Okay.
嗯。

Ted: And you? You've probably had a wonderful summer doing wonderful things.

你呢？你應該做了很多精彩的事，有個很棒的夏天。

Bill: Why do you say it like that?

你為什麼那樣說？

Ted: I talked to Kara and Anne.

我跟卡拉和安妮聊過。

Bill: Yes?

真的嗎？

Ted: They both gave me a speech about how wonderful their summers were.

她們兩個都把我訓了一頓，說她們暑假玩得多開心。

Bill: The only reason they lectured you is because they care about you.

她們訓你一頓，是因為她們關心你。

Ted: Uh huh.

嗯。

Bill: They both worry about you spending too much time online.

她們都擔心你花了太多時間上網。

Ted: Right.
對。

Bill: They worry about you not living your life. There's more to life than computers.
她們擔心你沒有好好過生活，人生不只是電腦而已。

Ted: I have been spending too much time on the computer.
我花太多時間在電腦上了。

Bill: You have?
是嗎？

Ted: I've been spending too much time emailing and surfing and chatting.
我花太多時間發電子郵件、瀏覽網際網路，和聊天。

Bill: You think so?
你真的這麼認為？

Ted: I haven't been spending enough time with my friends.
我和朋友在一起的時間不夠。

Bill: You mean that?
你真的這麼認為？

Ted: Yes. My email hobby has become a full

Chapter 1
Chapter 2
Chapter 3
Chapter 4
Chapter 5
Chapter 6
Chapter 7
Chapter 8
Chapter 9
Chapter 10

time job. I'm not even getting paid for it.

真的。我對電子郵件的興趣成了我的全職工作，甚至還沒錢賺呢。

Bill: Yes.

是啊。

Ted: I can't remember the last time I went bowling or to a movie.

我都不記得自己上次去打保齡球、看電影，是什麼時候的事了。

Bill: I know.

我了解。

Ted: I can't remember the last time I had a good conversation like right now.

我也不記得上次像這樣愉快談天，是什麼時候了。

Bill: This is a good conversation. It's a good conversation between good friends.

我們確實談得很愉快，而且還是好朋友之間的愉快談天。

Ted: Yes.

沒錯。

Bill: It's nice to have you back Ted. Do you

want to go get some pizza?
真高興你又回來了，泰德。要不要去吃披薩？

Ted: I'd love to. Are you buying?
當然好，你要請客嗎？

Bill: No, Ted. You are.
不，是你請客，泰德。

Ted: Darn it. Some friend you are. My computer doesn't make me pay for pizza.
拜託，這算哪門子的朋友。我的電腦就不會叫我出錢買披薩。

Bill: Ted!
泰德！

Ted: I'm joking! Just joking. Let's go get pizza.
開玩笑，開玩笑的！我們去買披薩吧。

Chapter 1
Chapter 2
Chapter 3
Chapter 4
Chapter 5
Chapter 6
Chapter 7
Chapter 8
Chapter 9
Chapter 10

Questions 習題

____1. What are Bill and Ted doing as they talk?
   A) They are holding hands.
   B) They are doing dishes.
   C) They are going for a drive.
   D) They are going for a walk.

____2. Where are Bill and Ted walking to?
   A) They are just going to see where they end up.
   B) They are just going to see where they grew up.
   C) They are just going to see where they threw up.
   D) They are just going to see where they bought a pup.

____3. How are Bill and Ted getting along?
   A) Poorly
   B) Badly
   C) Good
   D) Not well

____(4)When are they going for pizza?
   A) Tomorrow
   B) Today
   C) Tonight
   D) Tuesday

__D__ 1.　比爾和泰德邊聊邊做什麼？

　　　A）他們正在握手。

　　　B）他們正在做菜。

　　　C）他們正要去開車。

　　　D）他們正要去散步。

__A__ 2.　比爾和泰德要走去哪裡？

　　　A）他們打算看看最後能走到哪兒。

　　　B）他們要去看他們長大的地方。

　　　C）他們要去看他們被丟掉的地方。

　　　D）他們要去看他們抱小狗的地方。

__C__ 3.　比爾和泰德處得如何？

　　　A）貧窮地

　　　B）拙劣地

　　　C）不錯

　　　D）不太好

Chapter

7

__B__ 4.　他們什麼時候要去買披薩？

　　　A）明天

　　　B）今天

　　　C）今晚

　　　D）星期二

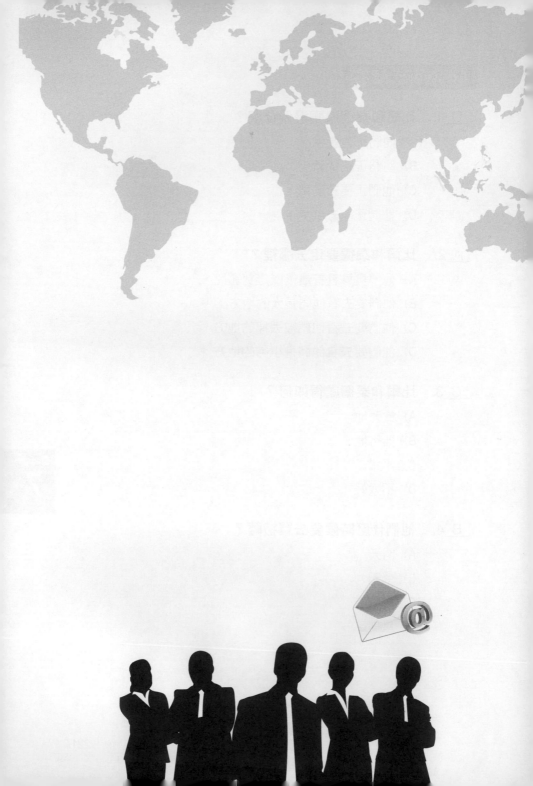

Chapter
8

ReUnited

歡喜團圓

Unit 1 Keeping in Touch
保持連繫

> Ted and Kara are eating supper in Kara's kitchen.
> 泰德和卡拉在她的廚房裡吃晚餐。

👤 Ted泰德　👤 Kara卡拉

Ted: Kara, will you pass the potatoes please?
卡拉，幫我拿馬鈴薯好嗎？

Kara: Yes, Ted. Here you go.
好啊，泰德，拿去。

Ted: Thanks. They're delicious.
謝啦，好好吃喔。

Kara: I'm glad that you like them.
我很高興你喜歡它們。

Ted: You're an excellent cook.
妳真會做菜。

Kara: I like to cook. I don't understand when people say they don't like to cook.

我喜歡做菜。我不懂為什麼有人不喜歡做菜。

Ted: I do.

我就不喜歡。

Kara: It's easy. Anybody can cook. It's fun.

做菜很簡單，誰都會的，很有趣。

Ted: I'm glad you like to cook. I'm also glad that you invited me over for supper.

真高興妳喜歡做菜，也謝謝妳請我來吃晚餐。

Kara: You're welcome.

不客氣。

Ted: The food is delicious.

東西好好吃。

Kara: Thanks. I'm glad that you're enjoying it.

謝謝，很高興你喜歡。

Ted: To you cooking's easy. I don't find it easy at all. I find it hard. I burn everything.

對妳來説，做菜很簡單。對我來説一點也不，我覺得好難。我把每樣東西都燒焦了。

Chapter 1

Chapter 2

Chapter 3

Chapter 4

Chapter 5

Chapter 6

Chapter 7

Chapter 8

Chapter 9

Chapter 10

Kara: I'm sure you don't.
你不會的。

Ted: I even burn water.
我連水都會燒乾。

Kara: You're just being funny. No one can burn water.
你是開玩笑的吧，沒有人會把水燒乾的。

Ted: Come over some time. I'll show you.
哪天妳來我家，我燒給妳看。

Kara: Eat your food. It's getting cold.
吃你的東西吧，菜要涼了。

Ted: Okay.
好。

Ted digs into his potatoes.
泰德埋著頭吃馬鈴薯。

Kara: I'm glad you've started coming out again. You're not stuck to your computer.
我很高興你不再待在家裡了，不再整天盯著電腦。

Ted: I was spending too much time emailing and not enough time with my friends.

我花太多時間在收發電子郵件，和朋友在一起的時間
不夠。

Kara: Yes.
對呀。

Ted: I wasn't spending enough time with my
family either.
也沒有好好陪伴家人。

Kara: Family is important. Everyone needs to
keep in touch with their family.
家人是很重要的，每個人都該和家人保持聯繫。

Ted: Yes.
對。

Kara: I talk to my Mom and Dad everyday.
我每天都和我爸媽聊天。

Ted: Everyday? Doesn't that cost a lot of
money?
每天？那不是要花很多錢嗎？

Kara: We keep in contact with email too. That
helps to keep the cost down. I phone
them every week so I get to hear their
voices. I feel closer to them. It's a better

Chapter
1

Chapter
2

Chapter
3

Chapter
4

Chapter
5

Chapter
6

Chapter
7

Chapter
8

Chapter
9

Chapter
10

visit than emailing.

我們也用電子郵件聯絡，那可以省一點錢。我每週打電話給他們，這樣才能聽到他們的聲音，會覺得比較親近。親自問候比傳電子郵件好。

Ted: I agree.

我同意。

Kara: When's the last time you talked to your mother?

你上次和你媽說話，是什麼時候的事了？

Ted: It's been a while. Too long. I should phone her.

好一陣子了，太久了。我該打個電話給她。

Kara: That's a good idea. I'm sure she'd love to hear from you.

好主意，她一定很想知道你的消息。

Ted: She doesn't have email. I'll have to phone her.

她沒有電子郵件，我必須打電話給她。

Kara: You can always write a letter. That doesn't cost a lot of money.

你可以寫信，花不了多少錢。

Ted: That's a good idea. It doesn't have to be a long letter.

好主意，不一定要寫很長。

Kara: Right.

對呀。

Ted: A quick note saying hi will do the trick. I could send a letter every week.

寫個短字條去打聲招呼也好，我可以每週寫一封。

Kara: Yes.

是的。

Ted: And phone her once a week. That'd be good.

然後每週打一通電話給她，這樣很好。

Kara: She'd be very happy.

她一定很高興的。

Ted: And I'd be very happy if you have any potatoes left.

如果妳還有馬鈴薯，我也會很高興的。

Kara: I do. Help yourself.

還有啊，自己來吧。

Chapter 1

Chapter 2

Chapter 3

Chapter 4

Chapter 5

Chapter 6

Chapter 7

Chapter 8

Chapter 9

Chapter 10

____1. What does Ted think of the potatoes?

   A) They are not bad.

   B) They are stale.

   C) They need some butter.

   D) They are delicious.

____2. How often does Kara keep in touch with her parents?

   A) Every week

   B) Every two weeks

   C) Every month

   D) She doesn't keep in touch with her parents.

____3. Who made supper?

   A) Kara's mother and father made supper.

   B) Kara made supper.

   C) Ted's mother made supper.

   D) Ted made supper.

____4. Why does Ted want Kara to come over?

   A) He can cook for her.

   B) He will show her that he burns water.

   C) He will burn supper for her.

   D) He will email her mother.

Answers 解答

<u>D</u> 1. **泰德覺得馬鈴薯如何？**

　　A）它們還不錯。

　　B）它們不新鮮。

　　C）它們需要加一些奶油。

　　D）它們很美味。

<u>A</u> 2. **卡拉多久和父母聯絡一次？**

　　A）每週

　　B）每兩週

　　C）每月

　　D）她沒有和她的父母保持聯絡。

<u>B</u> 3. **晚餐是誰做的？**

　　A）卡拉的媽媽和爸爸做晚餐。

　　B）卡拉做晚餐。

　　C）泰德的媽媽做晚餐。

　　D）泰德做晚餐。

<u>B</u> 4. **為何泰德要卡拉去他家？**

　　A）他可以為她煮菜。

　　B）他要向她展示，他如何把水燒乾。

　　C）他將為她把晚餐燒焦。

　　D）他將要寄電子郵件給她媽媽。

Chapter 8

Making up
你再掰呀

Ted and Anne are enjoying some chocolate cake in Anne's kitchen.
泰德和安妮在她家的廚房裡，吃著巧克力蛋糕。

  Anne安妮   Ted泰德

Anne: Are you telling the truth, Ted?
你是說真的嗎，泰德？

Ted: Yes, I am. I burn water.
真的，我會把水燒乾。

Anne: I think that you're making that up.
我覺得那是你瞎掰的。

Ted: I'm not. You should come over some time. I'll show you. I am that bad of a cook.
才沒有，妳有空過來，我做給妳看，我真的是一個很糟糕的廚師。

Anne: I love to bake. I bake all kinds of things.

I bake cookies, pies, and cakes.

我喜歡烘培。我做各式各樣的點心，像是餅乾、派和蛋糕。

Ted: I'm a terrible baker. I burn everything.

我很不會烘培，什麼都會烤焦。

Anne: I can't believe that you've burned water.

我不相信你會把水燒乾。

Ted: Your chocolate cake is terrific. Can I have another piece?

妳的巧克力蛋糕真好吃，我可不可以再吃一塊？

Anne: Of course. There's still a lot of cake left. Do you want ice cream on this piece?

當然，還有剩下好多蛋糕。要不要放些冰淇淋在上面？

Ted: Yes, please.

好的，謝謝。

Anne: I'm so glad that you're enjoying my cake.

我真高興你喜歡吃我的蛋糕。

Ted: I am.

我喜歡。

Anne: I'm also very glad that you and I have

Chapter 1

Chapter 2

Chapter 3

Chapter 4

Chapter 5

Chapter 6

Chapter 7

Chapter 8

Chapter 9

Chapter 10

made up.

我也很高興我們又和好了。

Ted: Me too. I didn't like when we had problems. I'm glad we've made up.

我也是，我不喜歡彼此不和，真高興我們又和好了。

Anne: It's fun being with you. It's good that you're spending less time on the computer.

和你在一起好有趣。你現在沒花那麼多時間在電腦上，真好。

Ted: Yes.

是啊。

Anne: I get fewer emails from you but I don't mind. I prefer talking to you.

我現在比較少收到你的電子郵件，但沒關係，我比較喜歡和你說話。

Ted: I have a better visit on the phone or in person. I get to see you and hear your voice.

我現在較常打電話或見面，這樣可以看到妳或聽見妳的聲音。

Anne: You should eat your cake. Your ice cream is melting.

你快點吃你的蛋糕。你的冰淇淋溶化了。

Ted: Did you know that melted ice cream is bad for you?

妳知不知道溶化的冰淇淋對身體不好？

Anne: No. I didn't know that.

我不知道。

Ted: Melted ice cream is dangerous for your health.

溶化的冰淇淋有害健康。

Anne: It is not.

不會吧。

Ted: I read it in the paper. They just learned that melted ice cream is bad for the heart.

我在報上看到的。最近的發現指出，溶化的冰淇淋對心臟不好。

Anne: Are you serious?

真的還是假的？

Ted: Yes. Scientists have discovered that melted ice cream can cause a heart attack.

Chapter 1
Chapter 2
Chapter 3
Chapter 4
Chapter 5
Chapter 6
Chapter 7
Chapter 8
Chapter 9
Chapter 10

真的。科學家發現溶化的冰淇淋會引起心臟病。

Anne: I can't believe it.
我不相信。

Ted: No? Okay, then.
不相信？那算了。

Anne: What do you mean?
你這話什麼意思？

Ted: It is okay if you don't believe it.
妳不相信沒關係。

Anne: Why?
為什麼呢？

Ted: Because I made it up. Everybody knows that melted ice cream is safe to eat.
因為那是我掰的，誰都知道溶化的冰淇淋，吃了沒問題。

Anne: Ted?
泰德？

Ted: Yes, Anne?
怎麼啦，安妮？

Anne: No more cake and ice cream for you.

Better safe than sorry.
不准吃蛋糕和冰淇淋了。安全總比後悔好。

Ted: What?
什麼？

Anne: Just in case it is bad for your heart.
免得你吃了對心臟不好。

Ted: Darn it.
可惡。

Chapter 1
Chapter 2
Chapter 3
Chapter 4
Chapter 5
Chapter 6
Chapter 7
Chapter 8
Chapter 9
Chapter 10

____1. Why does Ted want another piece of chocolate cake?

        A) It is good.

        B) It is very good.

        C) It is great.

        D) It is delicious.

____2. Who is melted ice cream bad for?

        A) Everybody

        B) Nobody

        C) Scientists

        D) Ted

____3. What does Anne like to do?

        A) Take food away from Ted.

    B) Bake

        C) Burn water

        D) Melt ice cream

____4. Where are Anne and Ted eating cake and ice cream?

        A) At Anne's place

        B) It does not say.

        C) At Ted's place

        D) Both A and C are correct.

 D 1. **為什麼泰德還要一塊巧克力蛋糕？**
A）好吃。
B）很好吃。
C）很棒。
D）很美味。

 B 2. **溶化的冰淇淋對誰不好？**
A）每個人
B）沒有人
C）科學家
D）泰德

 B 3. **安妮喜歡做什麼？**
A）從泰德那裡拿走食物。
B）烘培
C）把水燒乾
D）溶解冰淇淋

 A 4. **安妮和泰德在哪裡吃蛋糕和冰淇淋？**
A）在安妮家
B）沒有說。
C）在泰德家
D）A和C皆正確。

Chapter
8

Vocabulary 字彙通

| melt | v. | 融化 |

An Excellent Adventure

超級探險

Bill and Ted are waiting for the bus.
比爾和泰德在等公車。

👤 Bill比爾　👤 Ted泰德

Bill: This was a good idea. I've never done this before. I like to try new things.
這個主意很好，我從來沒做過這種事，我喜歡新鮮事。

Ted: I'm excited. I've never done this before either. It'll be fun.
我好興奮，從來沒做過這種事，好有趣。

Bill: Where did you hear about this flea market?
你從哪裡聽說有這個跳蚤市場的？

Ted: I read about it in the newspaper. I've always wanted to go to a flea market.
在報上看到的。我一直想去跳蚤市場。

Bill: I've never heard of a flea market before. Tell me again what it is.

我以前也聽過跳蚤市場，再跟我講講那是什麼樣的地方。

Ted: A flea market is where people bring used things they do not want any more.

很多人會把不用的舊東西，拿去跳蚤市場。

Bill: Okay.

嗯。

Ted: They sell them instead of throwing them away.

他們不是把東西丟掉，而是拿去賣。

Bill: What do people sell at a flea market?

他們在跳蚤市場裡賣些什麼呢？

Ted: They sell furniture, dishes, toys and clothes.

賣家具、鍋碗瓢盆、玩具和衣服。

Bill: Yes?

真的？

Ted: They sell almost anything you can find in a house.

幾乎任何家用物品都可以賣。

Chapter 1

Chapter 2

Chapter 3

Chapter 4

Chapter 5

Chapter 6

Chapter 7

Chapter 8

Chapter 9

Chapter 10

Bill: When my Dad gets a new table and chairs he can sell the old ones at a flea market?

要是我爸爸買新桌椅，就可以把舊的拿到跳蚤市場賣嗎？

Ted: He gets a little money and someone gets a table and chairs that doesn't cost a lot.

他可以賺一點錢，而別人也不用花很多錢，就可以買到一套桌椅。

Bill: Will there be food there? I didn't have breakfast this morning. I'm hungry.

那裡有吃的嗎？我早上還沒吃早餐，肚子餓了。

Ted: There will be food. You'll be able to buy a drink and a hot dog or a cookie.

那裡有吃的。你可以買飲料、熱狗或餅乾。

Bill: Good.

真好。

Bill's stomach rumbles.
比爾的肚子咕嚕咕嚕叫。

Ted: You can buy homemade baking and take

it home with you.
你可以買手工餅乾帶回家。

Bill: Do you think that someone will sell pie? I like pie.
你覺得會有人賣派嗎？我喜歡派。

Ted: Some people make things to sell. Pies sell well. So do cookies and cakes.
有些人會做東西來賣。派的生意很好，餅乾蛋糕也是。

Bill: I bet.
一定是。

Ted: People sell vegetables they grow. Some sew clothes and make toys.
有些人賣自己種的青菜，有些做衣服或玩具。

Bill: Interesting.
真有趣。

Ted: There will be old and new things for you to look at and buy.
你可以看到或買到新的和舊的東西。

Bill: I'd like to find a bike. Do you think someone might have a bike for sale?
我想找腳踏車，你覺得會有人賣腳踏車嗎？

Chapter
1

Chapter
2

Chapter
3

Chapter
4

Chapter
5

Chapter
6

Chapter
7

Chapter
8

Chapter
9

Chapter
10

Ted: It's possible. You never know. We'll see. I'd like to find a desk.

可能啊，誰曉得呢，去看看吧。我想找個書桌。

Bill: What an excellent adventure.

好棒的探險啊。

Ted: This is much better than any adventure game you can play on the computer.

這比電腦上任何探險遊戲都好玩。

Bill: I've played those games. It's fun for a while. If I play too much I get a headache.

我玩過電玩，一開始很有趣，但是玩多了會頭痛。

Ted: It's more fun to have real adventures.

真實的探險更有趣。

Bill: Yes.

沒錯。

Ted: Playing on the computer, you don't leave the house. That's not a real adventure.

玩電動不能出門，不算真的探險。

Bill: A real adventure is easy to have. Any time you try something new is an adventure.

真的探險很簡單，嘗試新鮮事就是探險。

Ted: I'm glad to be sharing this adventure with you.

真高興和你一起探險。

Bill: I'm Bill and this is Ted and this is our excellent adventure!

我是比爾，這位是泰德，這是我們的超級探險！

Chapter
1

Chapter
2

Chapter
3

Chapter
4

Chapter
5

Chapter
6

Chapter
7

Chapter
8

Chapter
9

Chapter
10

___1. Why is Bill hungry?

A) He did not have breakfast.

B) He ate too much pie.

C) He had a drink, a hot dog, and a cookie.

D) Ted is a terrible cook.

___2. Who is getting a new kitchen table and chairs?

A) Ted

B) Bill

C) Bill and Ted

D) Bill's father

___3. What does Bill want to buy?

A) A kitchen table and chairs

B) A bicycle

C) Furniture, dishes, toys, and clothes

D) A desk

___4. When are Ted and Bill going to the flea market?

A) This afternoon

B) This evening

C) This morning

D) They are not going.

 A 1. **為什麼比爾餓了？**

   A）他沒有吃早餐。

   B）他吃了太多派。

   C）他喝了一杯飲料、吃了一支熱狗和一塊餅乾。

   D）泰德是差勁的廚師。

 D 2. **誰要買新的餐桌椅？**

   A）泰德

   B）比爾

   C）比爾和泰德

   D）比爾的爸爸

 B 3. **比爾要買什麼？**

   A）一張餐桌和椅子

   B）一輛腳踏車

   C）家具、餐具、玩具和衣服

   D）一張書桌

 C 4. **泰德和比爾何時要去跳蚤市場？**

   A）今天下午

   B）今天傍晚

   C）今天早上

   D）他們不要去。

Chapter
8

Vocabulary 字彙通

flea market	n.	跳蚤市場
rumble	v.	發咕嚕聲
sew	v.	縫製

Chapter

9

Growing Wiser

變聰明了

Learn Your Lesson
學習新東西

Anne and Bill are shopping for clothes.
安妮和比爾在買衣服。

 Anne安妮  Bill比爾

Anne: Did you have a nice time with Ted the other day, Bill?
比爾，前幾天你和泰德玩得高興嗎？

Bill: Yes, I did, Anne.
高興啊，安妮。

Anne: What did you do?
你們做了些什麼？

Bill: We went to a flea market.
我們去跳蚤市場。

Anne: I like flea markets. You can buy almost anything there.

我喜歡跳蚤市場，幾乎什麼都買得到。

Bill: You can get a good deal because people sell used things.

你可以撿便宜，因為大家賣舊貨。

Anne: You can buy homemade things like baking, garden vegetables, clothing, and toys.

你還可以買手工做的東西，像烘培點心、自家種的蔬菜、衣服、玩具等。

Bill: Yes.

對啊。

Anne: I buy vegetables at the flea market and I make soup with them.

我會去跳蚤市場買青菜回來煮湯。

Bill: I'd love to try your soup.

好想喝妳煮的湯。

Anne: I'll have you over next time I make some. You can come when I go buy veggies.

下次我煮的時候再請你來，我有去買青菜時，你就可以來。

Bill: Okay. I'd never been to a flea market

Chapter 1
Chapter 2
Chapter 3
Chapter 4
Chapter 5
Chapter 6
Chapter 7
Chapter 8
Chapter 9
Chapter 10

before. It was fun.
好啊。我從來沒去過跳蚤市場，好有趣。

Anne: Did you buy something?
你有買東西嗎？

Bill: Yes. I bought a bike.
有，我買了一輛腳踏車。

Anne: Is it in good shape?
腳踏車狀況還好嗎？

Bill: Yes. The man who owned the bike before took care of it.
嗯，車主保養得還不錯。

Anne: Did you get a good price?
便宜嗎？

Bill: Yes. I'd have paid much more money if I'd bought a new bike from a store.
便宜，如果我去店裡買，就貴得多了。

Anne: It's good that you have a bike. Now you and I can go bike riding together.
你有腳踏車真好，這樣我們可以一起去騎腳踏車。

Bill: Sure.
當然。

Anne: I love to ride my bike in the park. There are some nice bike paths in the park.
我喜歡在公園騎腳踏車，裡面有一些不錯的腳踏車專用道。

Bill: I'd like to go bike riding with you. I'm not very good yet. I'm still learning.
我想和妳一起去騎腳踏車，可是我還不太會，還在學。

Anne: That's okay. When you're ready, we'll go bike riding together.
那好，等你會騎了，我們就一起去。

Bill: Good.
好啊。

Anne looks at a pair of pants.
安妮正在看一條長褲。

Anne: I'm also learning something.
我還在學另一樣東西。

Bill: What are you learning?
妳在學什麼？

Anne: I'm learning how to dance.

Chapter 1
Chapter 2
Chapter 3
Chapter 4
Chapter 5
Chapter 6
Chapter 7
Chapter 8
Chapter 9
Chapter 10

我在學跳舞。

Bill: You're taking dance lessons?
妳在上舞蹈課？

Anne: Yes, I am.
嗯。

Bill: I'm a very good dancer. I love to dance.
我很會跳舞，我喜歡跳舞。

Anne: I'm taking dance lessons and you're learning how to ride your bike.
我在學跳舞，你在學腳踏車。

Bill: Maybe we could teach each other.
也許我們可以互相教導。

Anne: That is a good idea.
好主意。

Bill: There's someone else who's learning a lesson.
還有一個人也在學東西。

Anne: Who's that?
誰啊？

Bill: Ted. He's learning that he likes to spend

time with his friends more than emailing.

泰德，他在學習多陪朋友、少發電子郵件。

Anne: Good.

很好。

Bill: He's learning that he needs to spend time with his friends or he might lose them.

他在學習多花一點時間在朋友身上，免得失去他們。

Anne: Maybe he'd like to learn how to dance and ride a bike. That would be more fun.

他可能也想學跳舞和騎腳踏車，那就更有趣了。

Bill: I agree with you. Let's email him and ask him to join us.

我同意。我們發電子郵件給他，看他要不要參加。

Anne: Okay but I think that it'll be easier to reach him if we phone.

好，不過我想打電話比較容易找到他。

Bill: These days, yes.

沒錯，最近都是這樣。

Chapter
1

Chapter
2

Chapter
3

Chapter
4

Chapter
5

Chapter
6

Chapter
7

Chapter
8

Chapter
9

Chapter
10

___1. Where does Anne like to ride her bike?
A) In the park
B) At the flea market
C) While she is buying vegetables
D) While she is baking

___2. How does Anne know how to dance?
A) She read a book.
B) She watched a TV show.
C) She is taking lessons.
D) Kara is teaching her.

___3. Why does Bill want Anne to invite him over?
A) He wants to send email from her computer.
B) He wants to use her phone.
C) He wants to take her to the flea market.
D) He wants to try her soup.

___4. Who is learning how to ride a bike?
A) Anne is learning how to ride.
B) Bill is learning how to ride.
C) Ted is learning how to ride.
D) Anne and Bill are learning how to ride.

 A 1.　**安妮喜歡去哪裡騎腳踏車？**

　　A）公園裡

　　B）跳蚤市場裡

　　C）當她買菜時

　　D）當她烘焙時

 C 2.　**安妮怎麼會跳舞？**

　　A）她讀了一本書。

　　B）她看了一個電視節目。

　　C）她正在上課。

　　D）卡拉在教她。

 D 3.　**為何比爾要安妮請他去她家？**

　　A）他要從她的電腦寄出電子郵件。

　　B）他要用她的電話。

　　C）他要帶她去跳蚤市場。

　　D）他要去試喝她的湯。

 B 4.　**誰在學騎腳踏車？**

　　A）安妮在學怎麼騎。

　　B）比爾在學怎麼騎。

　　C）泰德在學怎麼騎。

　　D）安妮和比爾在學怎麼騎。

Chapter
9

Who'd Have Thought
誰料想得到

Kara is trying to sell some homemade cooking on a table on the street outside her apartment.
卡拉在公寓外的街上擺了張桌子，來賣她做的手工餅乾。

 Anne安妮　 Kara卡拉

Anne: Kara, what are you doing?
卡拉，妳在做什麼？

Kara: Hi, Anne. I'm trying to sell my cooking.
嗨，安妮，我在試著賣自己做的食物。

Anne: Why are you doing that?
為什麼要這樣做呢？

Kara: The boys told me about the flea market. People sell their homemade baking there?
那些男生們談到跳蚤市場，有人賣自己做的烘培點心，是嗎？

Anne: Yes.
是啊。

Kara: I don't bake much but I do like to cook. I'm a good cook.
我不常做點心，但喜歡做吃的，我很會做菜。

Anne: Good for you.
這樣很不錯啊。

Kara: I need to make some extra money. I thought I'd sell my cooking.
我需要賺外快，我想來賣自己做的食物。

Anne: That might be a good idea. How's it going so far?
這可能是個不錯的主意，生意如何？

Kara: It's not going well. I don't know why.
不怎麼好，不知道為什麼。

Anne: Maybe you should move your table.
也許妳該移 一下桌子。

Kara: Why? What's wrong with where it is now?
為什麼？這裡有什麼不對嗎？

Anne: You didn't set up your table in a good

Chapter
1

Chapter
2

Chapter
3

Chapter
4

Chapter
5

Chapter
6

Chapter
7

Chapter
8

Chapter
9

Chapter
10

spot. You're right in front of a restaurant.

妳沒有把桌子擺在好地點，妳擺在一家餐廳前面。

Kara: Oh. I didn't notice. How embarrassing.

哦，我沒有注意到，真糗。

Anne: Here. I'll help you move your table. Let's move it under that tree.

來，我幫妳搬桌子，我們把它搬到那 樹底下。

Anne and Kara move the table under the tree and away from the restaurant.
安妮和卡拉把桌子搬離餐廳，移到樹下。

Kara: Thanks for helping me.

謝謝妳幫忙。

Anne: Maybe there's some other way that you can make extra money.

也許妳還有其他賺外快的方法。

Kara: I don't know what else to do. Do you have any ideas?

我不知道還能做什麼，妳有什麼點子嗎？

Anne: Kara, are you still painting?

卡拉，妳還在畫畫嗎？

Kara: Yes.
嗯。

Anne: You should sell your paintings. They're beautiful. You're a very good painter.
妳應該賣畫，它們都很漂亮，妳很會畫。

Kara: Thanks. I'd like to but I can't afford to open a store to sell my paintings.
謝謝，我也希望，但是我沒有錢開店、賣畫。

Anne: Can you find a store that will sell them for you?
妳能不能找到一家店幫妳寄賣呢？

Kara: I've tried but the stores won't give me a chance. I haven't sold any paintings yet.
我試過，但他們不給我機會，到現在一幅畫都沒賣過。

Anne: So?
然後呢？

Kara: They won't carry my paintings until I have sold some.
除非我賣過一些畫，否則他們不會幫我寄賣。

Anne: Why is that?
為什麼呢？

Chapter 1

Chapter 2

Chapter 3

Chapter 4

Chapter 5

Chapter 6

Chapter 7

Chapter 8

Chapter 9

Chapter 10

Kara: To prove that they'll sell. They're scared no one will buy them.

這樣才能保證銷得出去，他們怕沒人買。

Anne: The art stores will sell your paintings once they know that people will buy them?

如果美術社知道有人會買妳的畫，他們就會幫妳寄賣？

Kara: Yes.

是的。

Anne: Then we need to sell your paintings. I'll help you. We'll ask the boys to help too.

那我們就必須幫妳把畫賣出去。我幫妳，叫那些男生也來幫忙。

Kara: But how will we do it?

但要怎麼做呢？

Anne: Ted knows computers very well.

泰德很會電腦啊。

Kara: Yes he knows computers better than the rest of us do.

是啊，他比我們都懂。

Anne: We'll sell your paintings by computer.

我們用電腦來賣妳的畫。

Kara: You think we should sell my paintings on the Internet?

妳是說在網路上賣我的畫？

Anne: Yes. That's the easiest way to do it.

沒錯，那是最簡單的方法。

Kara: I think that's a great idea. Ted's computer skills will finally be useful.

這個點子真棒，泰德的電腦專長終於可以派上用場。

Anne: I never thought that I'd be happy about Ted being on the computer.

我從來沒想到，自己會很高興泰德的電腦很強。

Kara: Yes. Who would've thought that we'd want him to use his email skills?

沒錯，誰會想到，我們會需要他發揮電子郵件專長？

Chapter 1
Chapter 2
Chapter 3
Chapter 4
Chapter 5
Chapter 6
Chapter 7
Chapter 8
Chapter 9
Chapter 10

___1. Who is selling homemade cooking on
the street?
A) Anne
B) The restaurant
C) Kara
D) The flea market

___2. What are Kara and Anne going to sell
on the Internet?
A) Kara's cooking
B) Homemade baking
C) The restaurant
D) Kara's painting

___3. When did Kara move the table?
A) When Anne said it was in front of a res-
taurant
B) When Anne came over to the table
C) When Anne bought some cooking
D) When Anne stood under a tree

___4. Where did Kara and Anne move the table to?
A) Under a tree
B) In front of the restaurant
C) Into the restaurant
D) None of the above

 C 1. **誰在街上賣自己做的手工餅乾？**

A）安妮

B）餐廳

C）卡拉

D）跳蚤市場

 D 2. **卡拉和安妮要在網路上賣什麼？**

A）卡拉的餐點

B）手工餅乾

C）餐廳

D）卡拉的畫

 A 3. **卡拉何時移動桌子？**

A）當安妮說它在餐廳前面

B）當安妮走到桌旁

C）當安妮買一些點心來

D）當安妮站在樹下

 A 4. **卡拉和安妮把桌子搬到哪裡？**

A）樹下

B）餐廳前面

C）餐廳裡

D）以上皆非

Chapter
9

What Friends Are For
患難見真情

> Ted is visiting over at Kara's house.
> 泰德到卡拉家拜訪。

 Kara卡拉   Ted泰德

Kara: Ted, it's good of you to help me.
泰德，謝謝你過來幫我。

Ted: Kara, I'm glad to be able to help.
卡拉，我很高興能幫得上忙。

Kara: Who knew that your computer skills would end up being so important?
誰知道到頭來，你的電腦專長會變得這麼重要。

Ted: Yes.
是啊。

Kara: I feel bad for being angry with you for spending so much time online.

真對不起，我以前還氣你花太多時間上網。

Ted: Don't worry. I'm also happy that my email skills will help.
別這麼説，我也很高興我的電子郵件專長派得上用場。

Kara: Okay.
嗯。

Ted: You were right to be worried about me. I wasn't being a very good friend.
妳的擔心是對的，我以前那樣子不是一個好朋友。

Kara: But all that's changed.
你現在已經不一樣了。

Ted: I know now that computers and email are only useful tools.
我現在知道電腦和電子郵件都只是有用的工具。

Kara: They're going to be very useful for me.
它們會幫我很大的忙。

Ted: Where do you keep your paintings? I'd like to look at them.
妳的畫放在哪裡？我想看看。

Kara: I keep them in the basement. Come with

Chapter 1

Chapter 2

Chapter 3

Chapter 4

Chapter 5

Chapter 6

Chapter 7

Chapter 8

Chapter 9

Chapter 10

me and I will show them to you.
我把它們放在地下室。跟我來，我帶你去看。

Kara and Ted go downstairs.
卡拉和泰德走到地下室。

Ted: The more I know about your paintings;
the better I can describe them on the Net.
我越了解妳的畫，我越能在網路上好好形容它們。

Kara: There are lots. There are forty.
我有很多畫，有四十幅。

Ted: When do you have time to do so much
painting?
妳什麼時候有空畫了這麼多畫？

Kara: I take an art class at university. I do some
paintings in class.
我在大學修一門藝術課，在課堂裡畫了一些。

Ted: Yes.
嗯。

Kara: I also like to paint before I go to sleep. It
helps me to relax.
我也喜歡在睡覺前畫畫，可以幫助我放鬆。

Ted: I see. I used to go for a walk to help me sleep.

我懂了，我以前用散步來幫助入睡。

Kara: That's good.

很好啊。

Ted: Then I stopped going for walks and started surfing the Net to help me sleep.

後來我不散步，就開始上網來幫助入睡。

Kara: Did going online work better?

上網比較有用嗎？

Ted: No. Look at all these paintings. They're beautiful.

不會。妳看這些畫，好漂亮。

Kara: Thanks. I love to paint. It's what I want to do for a career.

謝謝。我喜歡畫畫，希望將來以此為業。

Ted: What do you like to paint?

妳喜歡畫什麼呢？

Kara: I like to paint pictures of animals.

我喜歡畫動物。

Chapter 1

Chapter 2

Chapter 3

Chapter 4

Chapter 5

Chapter 6

Chapter 7

Chapter 8

Chapter 9

Chapter 10

Ted: What are your favorite animals?
妳最喜歡什麼動物？

Kara: I like to paint cats. I paint house cats and wild cats. I like to paint lions and tigers.
我喜歡畫貓，家貓、野貓都畫。我也喜歡畫獅子、老虎。

Ted: Good to know. I'll find chat rooms that have something to do with animals.
太好了，我會去找一些和動物有關的聊天室。

Kara: Okay.
好啊。

Ted: I'll post to people who visit the chat rooms to see if they want to buy a painting.
我會把訊息傳給聊天室的人，看他們要不要買畫。

Kara: Ted, that's a very good idea. You're a good friend for helping me.
好主意，泰德。你真是一個熱心幫忙的好朋友。

Ted: I already told you. I'm glad to help you, Kara. That's what friends are for.
我說過了，我很樂意幫妳，卡拉。朋友就是要互相幫忙。

___1. Where does Kara keep her paintings?

A) In her bedroom

B) In the kitchen

C) Under her bed

D) In the basement

___2. How many paintings does Kara have?

A) Fourteen

B) Forty

C) Four

D) Forty-four

___3. Why is Ted happy to help Kara?

A) He owes her a favor.

B) That's what friends are for.

C) She let him go in the basement.

D) She owes him a favor.

___4. Who might want Kara's paintings?

A) People who like Ted

B) People who like Kara

C) People who like to cook

D) People who like animals

Chapter
9

Answers 解答

__D__ 1.　卡拉把畫放在哪裡？

    A）她的臥室裡

    B）廚房裡

    C）床底下

    D）地下室裡

__B__ 2.　卡拉有多少幅畫？

    A）十四

    B）四十

    C）四

    D）四十四

__B__ 3.　為何泰德樂意幫助卡拉？

    A）他欠她人情。

    B）朋友就該如此。

    C）她讓他走到地下室。

    D）她欠他人情。

__D__ 4.　誰可能會買卡拉的畫？

    A）喜歡泰德的人

    B）喜歡卡拉的人

    C）喜歡煮飯的人

    D）喜歡動物的人

Chapter
10

All's Well That Ends Well

皆大歡喜

Business is Booming
生意興旺

Anne and Bill are walking to Anne's car.

安妮和比爾往她的車走去。

👤 Anne安妮　👤 Bill比爾

Anne: Bill, did you get my email? Kara's paintings are starting to sell.

比爾，你有沒有收到我的電子郵件？卡拉的畫開始賣了。

Bill: I did. That's great news. Where are they selling?

收到了，真是好消息。它們在哪裡賣？

Anne: Online. Can you believe it?

在網路上，你相信嗎？

Bill: How are they being sold online? Did Ted create a website for Kara?

上網怎麼賣？泰德幫卡拉架了一個網站嗎？

Anne: No. Ted's been auctioning Kara's paintings by email on the Net.

沒有，泰德在網路上用電子郵件幫卡拉拍賣畫作。

Bill: His email skills sure have come in handy.

他的電子郵件專長的確派上了用場。

Anne: He had good teachers.

因為他有好老師。

Bill: We were good teachers but you know he's much better at email and such.

我們是好老師沒錯，但他發電子郵件之類的本領比我們好多了。

Anne: The student has become much better than his teachers.

青出於藍嘛。

Bill: Tell me more about the auction.

再跟我說說拍賣的事。

Anne: He emails a picture of the painting to people who might be interested.

他把畫作的照片寄給那些可能會有興趣的人。

Bill: Yes.

嗯。

Anne: He gets them to email him what they would pay for it.

他讓那些人回信告訴他，願意付多少價格買畫。

Bill: Yes.

嗯。

Anne: He keeps telling people who are interested what other people are willing to pay.

他不斷告訴那些想買的人，有別人願意出更多的錢。

Bill: He makes them out bid each other.

他讓他們彼此競標。

Anne: Everybody is willing to pay more and more money.

每個人的價格都愈出愈高。

Bill: That's great. How many paintings has he sold?

太好了，他賣了幾幅？

Anne: Two.

兩幅。

Bill: That's it? That's not very good. You were so happy.

就這樣？那不怎麼好。妳還這麼高興。

Anne: I am. It's great.
是啊，這樣很棒啊。

Bill: I thought you were going to tell me he'd sold more than that. That's too bad.
我以為妳要說他賣了很多幅畫。真糟糕。

Anne: No, it's not.
不會呀。

Bill: I hope Kara's not upset. How much did he sell them for?
希望卡拉不會很失望。他賣了多少錢？

Anne: Nine hundred dollars US each.
每幅九百美元。

Bill: Are you serious? Nine hundred dollars... American? Each?
你說真的？九百……美元？一幅？

Anne: Yes.
是啊。

Bill: That's the best news I've heard all day. Ted's doing a great job.
這是我今天聽到最讚的消息，泰德真是太厲害了。

Chapter 1

Chapter 2

Chapter 3

Chapter 4

Chapter 5

Chapter 6

Chapter 7

Chapter 8

Chapter 9

Chapter 10

Anne: Yes.
是的。

Bill: That's a lot of money. Kara must be very happy.
那可是一大筆錢，卡拉一定很高興。

Anne: Kara is very happy. She really needed some extra money and now she has it.
卡拉非常高興，她很需要一筆外快，現在她賺到了。

Bill: What does she need extra money for?
她要外快做什麼？

Anne: I don't know. She hasn't told me but I'm sure it's for a good reason.
不知道，她沒告訴我，不過一定有什麼原因。

Bill: Yes. I'm sure that you're right. Well, this is a happy ending.
嗯，我想妳説的沒錯。這可是圓滿的結局。

Anne: It's not the end.
還不止這樣呢。

Bill: No?
怎麼説？

Chapter
1

Chapter
2

Chapter
3

Chapter
4

Chapter
5

Chapter
6

Chapter
7

Chapter
8

Chapter
9

Chapter
10

> Anne and Bill get to the car. Anne unlocks the car door.
> 安妮和比爾來到車子邊，安妮打開車門。

Anne: Ted is having such a good time that he's going to keep doing it.
泰德玩上癮了，他還要繼續下去。

Bill: Good for him.
不錯嘛。

Anne: Yes. He's decided to make a career out of his online skills.
是啊，他決定用他上網的本事來創業。

Bill: Maybe he can sell more paintings.
也許他可以賣更多畫。

Anne: Maybe. That'd be good. Kara would have lots of extra money.
也許。那會很好，卡拉可以賺更多外快。

Bill: Then maybe some of the art stores will want to sell her paintings.
或許會有美術社想賣她的畫。

Anne: Yes. They'd know that her paintings would sell.
對，他們就會知道她的畫賣得出去。

Bill: This makes me happy. Kara is a good friend and she deserves this.

真高興。卡拉是一個很好的朋友，這是她應得的。

Anne: And I'm sure it makes Ted feel good to help her so much.

而且我確定泰德很高興可以幫她這麼多忙。

Bill: Let's go find Ted and Kara and take them out for breakfast to celebrate.

我們找泰德和卡拉出來，一起吃早餐慶祝吧。

Anne: Are you going to buy my breakfast?

你要請我吃早餐嗎？

Bill: Do I have to?

一定要嗎？

Anne: Do you want to me to give you a ride to the restaurant or do you want to walk?

你要我載你到餐廳，還是走路去？

Bill: Anne can I buy your breakfast for you?

安妮，我可以請妳吃早餐嗎？

Anne: What a good friend you are. Yes, you can buy me breakfast. Nice of you to offer.

你真是一個好朋友。好吧，我讓你請吃早餐，你真好。

____1. How many paintings have been sold?

A) Nine hundred paintings have been sold.

B) Two hundred paintings have been sold.

C) Two paintings have been sold.

D) Nine paintings have been sold.

____2. Why is Bill paying for Anne's breakfast?

A) He wants a ride to the restaurant.

B) He is not buying Kara's breakfast.

C) He is buying Anne's breakfast.

D) Both B and C are correct.

____3. Who will come to breakfast?

A) Anne will come to breakfast.

B) Anne and Bill will come to breakfast

C) Anne, Bill and Ted will come to breakfast.

D) Anne, Bill, Ted, and Kara will go to breakfast.

____4. What is Ted selling by email?

A) Ted is selling breakfast by email.

B) Ted is selling paintings by email.

C) Ted is selling websites by email.

D) Ted is selling nothing by email.

Chapter

10

Answers 解答

<u>C</u> 1. 已經賣出幾幅畫？

    A）已經賣出九百幅畫。

    B）已經賣出兩百幅畫。

    C）已經賣出兩幅畫。

    D）已經賣出九幅畫。

<u>A</u> 2. 為何比爾要請安妮吃早餐？

    A）他要搭車去餐廳。

    B）他沒有買卡拉的早餐。

    C）他在買安妮的早餐。

    D）B和C皆正確。

<u>D</u> 3. 誰會來吃早餐？

    A）安妮會來吃早餐。

    B）安妮和比爾會來吃早餐。

    C）安妮、比爾和泰德會來吃早餐。

    D）安妮、比爾、泰德和卡拉會去吃早餐。

<u>B</u> 4. 泰德用電子郵件賣什麼？

    A）泰德用電子郵件賣早餐。

    B）泰德用電子郵件賣畫。

    C）泰德用電子郵件賣網站。

    D）泰德沒有用電子郵件賣東西。

Chapter
1

Chapter
2

Chapter
3

Chapter
4

Chapter
5

Chapter
6

Chapter
7

Chapter
8

Chapter
9

Chapter
10

Unit 2　**Money for Nothing**
財源滾滾

Ted is buying a coffee. Bill joins him at the counter.
泰德在買咖啡，比爾在收銀台和他碰面。

🧍 Ted泰德　　🧍 Bill比爾

Ted: Bill, I'm happy to see you. Do you have time to join me for a coffee?
比爾，真高興看到你。有空和我喝杯咖啡嗎？

Bill: I have time, Ted. I'd like a coffee.
有啊，泰德，我想喝杯咖啡。

Ted: I'm tired. That's why I need the coffee.
我很累，所以想喝杯咖啡。

Bill: Why are you tired? Have you not been sleeping well?
為什麼很累？你沒睡好嗎？

Ted: No, I'm sleeping just fine. I just haven't had much time to sleep. I've been busy.
不，我睡得還好，只是沒多少時間睡覺，最近很忙。

Bill: What have you been busy with?
你在忙些什麼？

Ted: Selling Kara's paintings online has been taking a lot of my time.
上網幫卡拉賣畫，花了我很多時間。

Bill: I imagine.
可以想見。

Ted: I've got customers who live in different countries. I've been chatting with them.
我的客戶來自不同國家，我一直在和他們聊。

Bill: Yes.
嗯。

Ted: Sometimes I have to get up in the middle of the night to chat with them.
有時候我必須半夜爬起來和他們聊。

Bill: Is it worth it?
這樣值得嗎？

Ted: It's worth it. I've sold lots of paintings. I've been able to help out a friend.

值得。我賣了好多畫,這樣能幫助我的朋友。

Bill: Good work, Ted. You've found a good way to put your email skills to use.

幹得好,泰德。你找到好好運用你的電子郵件專長的方法了。

Ted: I have.

是的。

Bill: You use your computer skills to help Kara. Your skills are a useful tool.

你用電腦技能來幫助卡拉,這專長很有用。

Ted: Thank you, Bill.

比爾,謝謝你。

Bill: How many paintings have you sold for Kara?

你幫卡拉賣了幾幅畫?

Ted: Half of them.

一半了。

Bill: How many is that?

那是多少?

Chapter 1

Chapter 2

Chapter 3

Chapter 4

Chapter 5

Chapter 6

Chapter 7

Chapter 8

Chapter 9

Chapter 10

Ted: She had forty paintings.
她有四十幅。

Bill: You've sold twenty paintings? Ted, that's terrific. Kara must be very happy.
你已經賣了二十幅？太棒了，泰德，卡拉一定高興極了。

Ted: I haven't told her yet. It's a surprise. I took all the paintings out of her basement.
我還沒告訴她，想要給她一個驚喜。我把所有的畫都從她的地下室拿出來了。

Bill: Where'd you put them?
你把它們放在哪裡？

Ted: I put them at my house. She doesn't know how many I've sold.
放在我家。她不知道我賣了幾幅。

Bill: She'll be so pleased. She'll be so thankful. I'm so impressed Ted. That's terrific.
她一定會非常高興、非常感謝。我真的很驚訝，泰德，太棒了。

Ted: There's more good news.
還有別的好消息呢。

Chapter
1

Chapter
2

Chapter
3

Chapter
4

Chapter
5

Chapter
6

Chapter
7

Chapter
8

Chapter
9

Chapter
10

> Ted and Bill pay for their coffees.
> 泰德和比爾付咖啡錢。

Ted: I've found art stores that want to sell her paintings.
我發現有美術社願意賣她的畫。

Bill: Incredible.
不可思議。

Ted: Every painting she makes will have a store to go to.
她畫的每幅畫都有店要賣。

Bill: Terrific.
好極了。

Ted: Since so many paintings have sold these stores know that all of them will sell.
既然賣了這麼多幅畫，這些店知道所有的畫都賣得出去。

Bill: This is such good news. Thank goodness you learned how to use email.
這真是好消息，真要感謝你學會了怎麼用電子郵件。

Ted: Thank goodness I have friends who took the time to teach me.
要感謝有朋友花時間教我。

Bill: You bet.
那當然。

Ted: Even though I went through a tough time, it's all been worth it.
雖然辛苦，但是值得。

Bill: When are you going to share the good news with Kara?
你什麼時候要告訴卡拉這個好消息？

Ted: I'd like to go to her house this afternoon. Would you like to come?
我想今天下午去她家。你要一起來嗎？

Bill: Yes. I'd love to be there when you share the news with her.
好，我也希望在場，聽你和她分享這個好消息。

Ted: Good.
好啊。

Bill: I can't wait to see the look on her face.
我真等不及看她臉上的表情。

Ted: Well, let's get our coffees to go. We'll go there right now.
好吧，我們把咖啡外帶，現在就去。

___1. How is Ted feeling?
A) Ted is sad.
B) Ted is angry.
C) Ted is tired.
D) Ted is bored.

___2. Why hasn't Ted been sleeping?
A) He has to get up in the middle of the night.
B) He just can't sleep.
C) He drinks too much coffee.
D) Kara has been asking questions.

___3. Who is going to Kara's house?
A) Ted
B) Ted and Bill
C) Ted, Bill, and Anne
D) No one is going to Kara's house.

___4. When will they tell Kara the news?
A) Tomorrow
B) Tuesday
C) Thursday
D) Today

Chapter
10

 C 1.　泰德感覺如何？

A）泰德在傷心。

B）泰德在生氣。

C）泰德覺得累。

D）泰德覺得無聊。

 A 2.　為什麼泰德沒有睡覺？

A）他必須在午夜起床。

B）他就是睡不著。

C）他喝太多咖啡。

D）卡拉被問問題。

 B 3.　誰要去卡拉家？

A）泰德

B）泰德和比爾

C）泰德、比爾和安妮

D）沒有人要去卡拉家。

 D 4.　他們何時要告訴卡拉這個消息？

A）明天

B）星期二

C）星期四

D）今天

Chapter
1

Chapter
2

Chapter
3

Chapter
4

Chapter
5

Chapter
6

Chapter
7

Chapter
8

Chapter
9

Chapter
10

Unit
3

What's It All For?
真相大白

Someone is knocking on Ted's door. He opens it to find Kara standing there.
有人在敲泰德家的門。他開門一看，卡拉站在那裡。

Ted泰德　　**Bill**比爾

Ted: Hi, Kara. What are you doing here?
嗨，卡拉，妳在這裡做什麼？

Kara: I want to thank you again for selling all of those paintings for me. I'm so happy.
我要再一次謝謝你幫我賣了那些畫，我真的好高興。

Ted: You're welcome.
不客氣。

Kara: It's like a dream come true.
那就好像是美夢成真。

Ted: I'm just happy to be able to help you. Like you helped me.
我很高興能幫妳，就像妳幫我一樣。

Kara: Yes?

真的？

Ted: Do you remember when I asked you to help me learn how to use email?

妳記不記得我請妳教我怎麼用電子郵件？

Kara: Yes.

記得。

Ted: Well, you helped me. Even when I was rude and difficult you helped me.

對啊，妳幫了我。即使我魯莽又難搞，但妳還是幫我。

Kara: Yes.

是啊。

Ted: You were a good friend. Now I've returned the favor.

妳是一個很好的朋友，我只是回報妳的恩惠。

Kara: Well, you've helped me more than I helped you.

你給我的幫忙，比我幫你的多太多了。

Ted: That's not true. You showed me that email is just a useful tool.

並沒有，妳讓我發現電子郵件只是一種有用的工具。

Kara: It's not a replacement for good friends.

它不是好朋友的替代品。

Ted: It's not a replacement for living life. You've helped me to lead a good life again.

也不是現實生活的替代品。妳幫我再度好好過生活。

Kara: Thank you, Ted.

謝謝你，泰德。

Ted: Will you answer a question for me?

妳可不可以回答我一個問題？

Kara: Yes.

可以。

Kara comes in and Ted shuts the door. They sit down in the living room.

卡拉進來，泰德把門關上。他們坐到客廳裡。

Ted: I don't know what you needed extra money for. Anne and Bill don't know either.

我不知道妳為什麼要賺外快，安妮和比爾也不知道。

Kara: That's right.

對。

Chapter 1
Chapter 2
Chapter 3
Chapter 4
Chapter 5
Chapter 6
Chapter 7
Chapter 8
Chapter 9
Chapter 10

Ted: Why did you need extra money?

為什麼妳要賺外快？

Kara: I wanted to tell all of you at the same time but I'll tell you now.

我本來想一起告訴你們，但我現在先告訴你。

Ted: Okay.

好啊。

Kara: You, Anne and Bill are my friends. I wanted to take you all on a vacation.

你、安妮和比爾都是我的朋友，我要帶你們一起去度假。

Ted: Really?

真的？

Kara: Bill, Anne and I went camping and you didn't get to come.

比爾，安妮和我上次有去露營，但你沒去。

Ted: Right.

對。

Kara: I wanted the extra money so that I could take the three of you on a camping trip.

我要賺外快，這樣才能帶你們三個一起去露營。

Ted: That's a nice surprise. I'd love to go camping with you.
這真是個驚喜，我很想跟你們一起去露營。

Kara: I don't want to go camping anymore.
但我不想去露營了。

Ted: Why not?
為什麼呢？

Kara: You made so much money for me. I want to do more than go camping.
你幫我賺了那麼多錢，我想要做露營更棒的事。

Ted: What do you want to do?
妳要做什麼？

Kara: I want to go to another country. I want to visit one of the best countries on earth.
我想出國，去世界上最棒的國家之一。

Ted: Canada?
加拿大？

Kara: Yes. I'm going to Canada.
對，我要去加拿大。

Ted: That's great, Kara. I've always wanted to

Chapter 1

Chapter 2

Chapter 3

Chapter 4

Chapter 5

Chapter 6

Chapter 7

Chapter 8

Chapter 9

Chapter 10

go there. Take lots of pictures for me.

太棒了，卡拉，我一直好想去那裡，幫我拍一堆照片回來。

Kara: No, Ted.

不，泰德。

Ted: Oh. Okay.

喔，好吧。

Kara: You can take lots of pictures. You're coming with me.

你可以自己照一堆照片，因為你要和我一起去。

Ted: Wow.

哇。

Kara: I want Anne and Bill to come with us too.

我要安妮和比爾也跟我們一起去。

Ted: I can't believe this.

我真不敢相信。

Kara: I have so much money that I can afford to pay for all of our trips to Canada.

我有這麼多錢，可以讓我們一起去加拿大玩。

Ted: This is great. I'm so happy. I'm so surprised.

太棒了，我好高興、好驚喜。

Kara: We're going to have so much fun.

我們一定會玩得很愉快。

Ted: When are you going to tell Anne and Bill?

我們什麼時候告訴安妮和比爾？

Kara: Let's go tell them now. Let's go tell them about the money and what it was all for.

現在就去告訴他們吧，告訴他們外快的來龍去脈。

Ted: Canada, here we come!

加拿大，我們來囉！

Chapter
1

Chapter
2

Chapter
3

Chapter
4

Chapter
5

Chapter
6

Chapter
7

Chapter
8

Chapter
9

Chapter
10

___1. What did Kara first want to do with the money?

A) She wanted to hide it.

B) She wanted to spend it on clothes.

C) She wanted to throw a big party.

D) She wanted to take her friends camping.

___2. When did Kara help Ted?

A) She helped him learn how to use email.

B) She helped him learn that email is just a useful tool.

C) She didn't help him learn anything.

D) A and B are correct.

___3. Where are the friends going?

A) They are going camping.

B) They are going to Canada.

C) They are going camping in Canada.

D) They are going bowling.

___4. Who will pay for the vacation?

A) Kara

B) Ted

C) Bill

D) Anne

Answers 解答

<u> D </u> 1. **卡拉最初要用這些錢做什麼？**

A）她要藏起來。

B）她要用來買衣服。

C）她要辦一個盛大的派對。

D）她要帶她的朋友去露營。

<u> D </u> 2. **卡拉何時幫助泰德？**

A）她幫助他學習如何使用電子郵件。

B）她幫助他學習把電子郵件變成有用的工具。

C）她沒有幫助他學習任何東西。

D）A和B皆正確。

<u> B </u> 3. **這幾個朋友要去哪裡？**

A）他們要去露營。

B）他們要去加拿大。

C）他們要去加拿大露營。

D）他們要去打保齡球。

<u> A </u> 4. **誰支付旅費？**

A）卡拉

B）泰德

C）比爾

D）安妮

Chapter
10

英語系列：16

Email英語會話與寫作技巧

作者／David Shih
出版者／哈福企業有限公司
地址／新北市中和區景新街 347 號 11 樓之 6
電話／(02) 2945-6285　傳真／(02) 2945-6986
郵政劃撥／31598840　戶名／哈福企業有限公司
出版日期／2015 年 5 月
定價／NT\$ 329 元（附 MP3）

全球華文國際市場總代理／采舍國際有限公司
地址／新北市中和區中山路 2 段 366 巷 10 號 3 樓
電話／(02) 8245-8786　傳真／(02) 8245-8718
網址／www.silkbook.com　新絲路華文網

香港澳門總經銷／和平圖書有限公司
地址／香港柴灣嘉業街 12 號百樂門大廈 17 樓
電話／(852) 2804-6687　傳真／(852) 2804-6409
定價／港幣 110 元（附 MP3）

email／haanet68@Gmail.com
網址／Haa-net.com
facebook／Haa-net 哈福網路商城

國家圖書館出版品預行編目資料

Email英語會話與寫作技巧／David Shih 著. -- 初版. -- 新
北市：哈福企業, 2015.05
　　面；　公分. --（英語系列；16）

　ISBN 978-986-5616-07-6（平裝附光碟片）

1.商業英文 2.會話 3.電子郵件

805.188　　　　　　　　　　　　　　　104007300